Never Even

Never Even

J. Kirsten Moe

Never Even

© J. Kirsten Moe 2018

This book is a work of fiction. Named locations are used fictitiously, and characters and incidents are the product of the author's imagination. Any resemblance to actual events or places or persons, living or dead, is entirely coincidental.

Published by
Lighthouse Christian Publishing
SAN 257-4330
5531 Dufferin Drive
Savage, Minnesota, 55378
United States of America

www.lighthousechristianpublishing.com

For Amber, Jade, Hunter and my 'kids' at Grand Meadow

Chapter One

I always enjoyed the walk to school on days like this but today I was especially exhilarated. Large oaks, elms, hickory, walnut and butternut trees stood like sentries lining the road. And down the bank a ways snaked the creek we knew as the Ottertail. Along its banks and in the lowlands lay smaller fields which were perfect for raising tobacco, the main cash crop of the day. Beyond these and up the bluff sides were the strip fields of corn and hay. Big branches arched over the lane creating a wooden canopy and a variety of birds sang overhead. Squirrels added their scratchy, scolding voices to the cacophony and darted out every so often. Above us, the sky was azure and sunbeams streamed through the leaves highlighted by the misty morning dew.

I was eager to get back to school to some kind of normal life. 'Normal' had evaded me since that March night in the sugar camp where I first met Emmit Romney. And it didn't end until the June night my sister Lila saved my life by shooting the outlaw. I had suffered a concussion and had been grazed by Romney's bullet. The remainder of my summer involved throbbing headaches, dizziness, and being sick to my stomach. Besides that, my best friend Willie Cooper wasn't around. After everything that happened, which amounted to him being nearly killed *twice* by the outlaw, his parents thought it best to send him far away for the remainder of the summer. He was put on a train bound for Montana to spend some time with an uncle who was a foreman on a cattle ranch.

I heard nothing until August when Willie's 'kinder' sister Betty told me he was on his way home. I was thrilled and counted the days until we could see each other and catch up. The truth was that I missed him terribly. But as soon as he returned, he was gone again for a week of Bible camp in the northern part of the state. Every other year I had gotten to go to camp too, but due to my headaches, my folks wouldn't let me go. I thought at least when he got back I would get to see him. But those hopes were soon dashed when Pastor Potter recruited him to go *back* to camp with a group of the men to remove some of the trees that had been damaged by a summer storm.

I hadn't seen my best friend for two months and that was hard. I couldn't remember a summer when we hadn't been together at least a couple of days every week, not counting Sundays, trading work, and sharing adventures. So my eagerness to get back to school and a 'normal life' were just a ruse for my real reason: I wanted to see Willie.

I took great care in getting ready the first morning back to school. I scrubbed until my skin was red, I brushed my hair until it shined, and I even wore a dress. And I never wore dresses to school! Grandma had given me a bottle of perfume for my thirteenth birthday. It was simply called 'Roses' and I applied it liberally.

We all had on new clothes. The boys wore new overalls and Lila wore a new skirt and top she had made as a 4-H project.

"Daddy said there's a new family on the Oliver place." She remarked.

My ten-year-old brother, Ben, who dreamed he would grow up to be a professional baseball player, picked up a stone and threw it as far as he could down the road. "Better have boys! We got enough girls around here."

"You can say that again!" Joe, Ben's twin, agreed. "What's the deal with you spending so much time in the bathroom, Hildi? There's other people that need to get in there, you know!"

"Mind your own business!" I growled.

"She had to fix up pretty." Ben tried to sound innocent, "Willie's back."

The boys followed me and I heard every word. I walked quicker, trying to get ahead of their words but I could still hear them.

"Oh, yeah," Joe replied, stretching out the words, "*now* I remember. You look *real nice*, Hildi."

"Yeah, and you smell good, too." That was followed by loud giggles.

"Like roses!"

I suppose I should have thanked them. After all, how many little brothers compliment their big sister on how she looks *and* smells, especially after she took twice as long in the bathroom? But then I got to thinking: maybe I'd applied too much 'Roses' perfume and that's what they were laughing about!

Lila did not try to catch up with me. I knew that even though we had become closer as sisters, the sore spot between us would always be Willie. That is, until one of us had a change of heart. Lila had admired my best friend ever since she was little. She always envied the relationship we shared. It was why she savored that week at camp without me. But it didn't bring all the benefits she thought it would.

***

Clang, Clang, Clang went the old schoolhouse bell. We had nearly thirty-five students within a two-mile radius who walked the hills and valleys to the little schoolhouse. It was located along the road of the wide, meandering valley of Ottertail Creek. The bluffs were tall. Nestled between them were narrow valleys with farms where folks eked out a humble existence. Ours was a valley farm. Yet, Granddad expanded it by buying up more land whenever he could. In total, we had close to 200 acres while the average farm was 160 or less. We raised jersey cattle, a few pigs, chickens, hay, corn and tobacco. On a farm no one has a chance to sit down for too long. There were always chores to be done, so we were all lean and strong.

We passed another long driveway which was similar to our own. At the end was the old Oliver farm. I wondered who the new occupants were and if they had children. The intersection gave us no clues, for the dirt there was just as dusty and untouched as where we walked. We could have easily seen any footprints coming from that house and there were none.

The valley opened up ahead. A large green field of tobacco was on one side of the road with our school on the other side. The schoolhouse was just off the road with a ball field out behind and Gundersons' cornfield bordering the school grounds.

Suddenly, we heard the roar of an engine behind us. We'd been walking up the middle of the road but scattered when the approaching car didn't slow down. A horn blared as it passed and the big man driving didn't seem to give us a second glance, but two of the three boys inside did. We were shaken. No one ever drove like that down our dirt roads unless it was an emergency and even then, they slowed down and gave folks a chance to get out of the way. Our once pristine clothes were now covered with a layer of dust and I felt it grind between my teeth. It surprised me when the big sedan turned into the schoolyard and someone got out. I was steamed. I didn't recognize the car or the driver and before we got to the school, the car had disappeared down the road.

"That was real nice!" I exclaimed sarcastically, trying to shake the dust out of my dress and hair.

Lila was at my side, "He didn't even slow down!"

"I know!"

We both spotted the passenger. He had his back to us. I was going to give him a piece of my mind.

"Hey! What do you think you're doing? No one around here drives like that! You could have killed us! You should have at least slowed down!" I yelled at his back.

He turned and I immediately saw a good-looking boy about my age with an amused look on his face, "You hillbillies don't need to take up the whole road. It's probably about time you learned to get to one side or the other. You never know, this little lesson mighta just saved your lives ... hick!"

And with that he turned away and went into the schoolhouse. I followed as I was not done with him. But Lila just stood there dumb and staring after this fellow. I was still angry, but I couldn't deny that he was impressive. He was taller than most of the boys, so I guessed that he might be even older than us. His blond hair was carefully combed and he was dressed well with what looked like store-bought clothes. Most of the kids at the Ottertail country school had hand-me-downs and clothes made by their mothers.

"Wait one minute!" I bellowed.

I started up the steps but Miss Hendricks, our teacher, stopped me at the door. "Hilda Barnum, what is the trouble? I could hear you all the way in here."

"We were just about run over. Miss Hendricks, this car didn't even slow down and *he* was in it."

"Excuse me, ma'am," the boy stepped up beside our teacher and was just as polite as could be, "*I* wasn't driving. That was my pop driving and he had a late start this morning. I've already told this young lady how sorry we are."

"There you have it," she said. "That ends the argument."

"But that's not what you just ... well it's no excuse! People around here ..."

"Hildi, I think you'd better cool off before you come inside." Miss Hendricks gave me the look she usually had reserved for trouble-makers. I knew not to cross her. Still, this new boy, whoever he was, had just lied and made me look like an idiot.

Lila still stood at the bottom of the steps looking star-struck. It was obvious that she thought his good looks excused his poor behavior.

"Who is that fella?" Ben and Joe looked as angry as me.

"Hildi, did you see him?" Finally, my sister spoke up.

I nodded and sat down beside the well pump.

"I've never seen eyes so blue!" she exclaimed.

Oh brother! I thought.

And that was my introduction to Andy Porter.

But my anger lasted only a minute. I looked up the road and in the distance I saw a familiar figure amongst many on their way to the schoolhouse. It was Willie Cooper. He wasn't in his usual bib-overalls, but I recognized the walk and his form. I was on my feet in an instant as I strained to see.

"You sure got a big smile on your face!" teased Joe.

I sat as quickly as I had stood. There it was again, that strange flutter in my stomach that started last March. It was getting harder to control my feelings. I didn't want things to change between Willie and me. I wanted us to always be best friends, no matter what. I watched him as he drew closer and tried to look past him as others entered the school yard. Norm ran up to the boys and showed them his baseball while Stella Johnson met Lila who quickly told her about the new boy with the blue eyes.

"How are you, Hildi?" asked Johnny Iverson who was in my class. He was tall, thin, and wore thick, horn-rimmed glasses.

"Hi, Johnny. I'm good. Did you have a nice summer?" I made polite conversation with the redheaded boy while I looked around him trying to see Willie.

"I broke my leg the first week of vacation and didn't get to do anything. It was awful. I got out of work but I couldn't swim for a month and you can't ride a bike in these hills with a cast on your leg. Say, Hildi, why are you so dressed up today? You smell really nice ..."

While Johnny talked on, Willie walked right past, up the steps, and into the schoolhouse.

Had he seen me? Was I being ignored? Maybe something *had* changed while he was away. I hadn't even gotten a good look at him.

The bell rang and everyone outside climbed the stairs and entered our one-room schoolhouse. Once inside, I spotted him. He had his back to me and I could see that he and the other boys were in animated conversation. His shoulders looked broad beneath the chambray shirt and instead of overalls, he wore blue jeans. I didn't want to interrupt but took the time to survey the room. There were a few new faces in the lower grades as well as some others who were closer to my age.

Miss Hendricks tapped her ruler lightly on the desk and we came to order. Within minutes she had us seated in rows according to grade level. As she did this, she introduced each new face. When she got to the boy whose father had nearly run us off the road, I paid particularly close attention.

"Andrew Porter is in eighth grade. His family is renting the Oliver house and will be attending school here this year. Andrew, would you tell the students a little about yourself?"

He stood and looked around at us, "I came from Ridgeview. My dad owns a construction company."

He sat down and Miss Hendricks looked at him, "And I understand you have a couple of brothers in high school."

"Yeah."

Miss Hendricks didn't correct his grammar, letting it slide for the time being. This Porter boy seemed a bit surly. I wondered how long it would take me to like him.

We recited the Pledge of Allegiance and the Lord's Prayer. It was the beginning of the first week of the new school year.

"Your first assignment this week is to write a theme: What I did during my summer vacation." Miss Hendricks wrote the subject of our theme on the chalkboard.

I usually jumped at a chance to write creatively, but not this time. I didn't have anything to write about. Except for that night at the mill in mid June, the rest of my summer had been completely uneventful. What made matters worse was that our teacher liked to have some of us read our themes in front of the class and I was *always* chosen to do this. As I thought about the theme, my love for writing and then sharing what I'd written, the sorrier I felt for myself.

"Now, please take out your pencils and paper. Grades four through eight will begin their themes," she directed and then began working with the lower grades.

I sat in the front of the classroom, the first person in the last row and unable to see anyone in my grade unless I turned around and looked. I wondered how many were eagerly getting out pencil and paper and how many were like me. I stared at the blackboard and Miss Hendricks' flowing handwriting upon it: What I did on my summer vacation ... what I did? I honestly didn't care about the assignment. Nor did I have anything to write.

What I did on my summer vacation: Nothing.

I wrote the sentence and stared at it. Miss Hendricks wouldn't like it. It was 9:45. Our school day started at 9:00 and ended at 4:00.

Only six hours and fifteen minutes and school would be out. The clock ticked and I doodled. I drew squares that I turned into houses and then added barns to which I added fences. Soon I had quite the little scene with a farmstead, a mill with a millwheel and millpond, trees, and hills. So intent was I in my drawing that I hadn't even heard the footsteps approaching.

"That's not the assignment," whispered a voice and I looked up to see Willie as he passed my desk on his way to the pencil sharpener. He slowed just long enough to make his comment. His eyes twinkled as they met mine and he turned back to carry out his task. I watched after him and smiled in spite of myself. My mind turned back to that June night outside the mill. I had looked up into those dark, twinkling eyes as he tended my head wound. We both smiled that night. That was the last time I'd seen him all summer. I spent that night in the hospital and then had to rest a few days at home. By the time I was ready to see anyone, Willie was on the train bound for Montana. I now looked forward to recess more than ever.

My class consisted of myself, Willie Cooper, Johnny Iverson, Barbara Bjornstad and Andy Porter. There were no more than five in each grade with some much smaller. Stella Johnson should have been in our class, but had rheumatic fever in first grade and missed so much school she was held back a year.

Our recess time was spent outside where we played Red Rover and Kick the Can. We had an hour for lunch and usually played baseball once a week until the snow fell. At 10:20 Miss Hendricks excused us. I didn't want to look too eager to speak to Willie, so I took my time putting things in my desk. But before I could get up Miss Hendricks was standing in front of me.

"Hildi, can we have a little talk?" she began, a good sign that she had used my nickname. If she had said 'Hilda' I would have been worried.

"Yes, ma'am?" I answered and began to stand.

But she motioned for me to keep my seat, "Are you feeling all right?"

This took me by surprise. Miss Hendricks lived with an elderly woman nearby during the school year, but over the summer she moved back to Prairie du Chien to stay with her parents. Although the news of Romney's escape and death would not have escaped her, I didn't think she was aware of everything that happened that June night.

"I understand you have had a lot of headaches this summer. I heard you had a very serious injury."

I nodded, "Yes, ma'am, but I'm fine now."

"Are you sure? If you need a rest let me know."

I took a deep breath, "Did my daddy talk to you?"

My father was on the school board and had been concerned about me all summer. Miss Hendricks smiled.

"He just wants me to be aware of what happened. What about Lila? How is she handling ... well, everything?"

I told her that Lila was doing fine. I did not tell her that, in fact, my sister had suffered terrible nightmares for weeks but seemed to be sleeping the night through now. By the time our 'little talk' was done, so was recess. Miss Hendricks left to ring the bell and the younger kids came scampering in. I stood up and crossed the room to look out the windows nearest the playground. The new boy, Andy Porter, was tossing little stones at the back of one of the third grade girls and when the child turned around he pretended to be in deep conversation with Norm Tucker.

Our blue sky was disappearing with a bank of clouds rising in the west and the air had turned sticky. When I turned back, I saw that Willie was standing near my desk and looking at me. He didn't say anything. He just stood there with the faintest smile on his face.

"What?" I said finally.

He shook his head and looked me up and down, "You're wearing a *dress*, Hildi. It ain't even Sunday!"

"So, I'm wearing a dress."

"Well," he began, "you look real nice. And is that roses I smell?"

My face was suddenly hot and I knew I was blushing.

"So," he looked very serious, "are you gonna dress this way from now on?"

I was thinking that I hadn't planned to, but if I was going to get this kind of reaction from him, that I just might.

"Why?" I queried.

He took a couple of steps towards me and my heart began to race.

"Well," he said again, "it's just that I was telling Andy about our baseball games and that you were one of our best hitters. Do you think you can play that good in a dress? I think sliding into home plate might be a problem."

"Oh," I said.

Miss Hendricks had returned but she wasn't alone. Chet Cooper was with her. He gestured at his son to meet him.

"There's a threat of a storm, son. We've got half an acre of tobacco to get in, so you'll have to come with me." Chet had come right from the field. His hands were black from the dirt and tobacco juice that mingles when one goes through the field cutting the stalks and laying down the rows. I could see the thick hair on his arms was sticky and his dungarees were stiff with the same combination of dirt and juice.

"Take your math home tonight and do the first fifteen problems on page eight," Miss Hendricks directed, "and don't forget to work on your theme."

The rest of the day grew heavy with humidity. The hours passed slowly until noon, when we all sat outside and ate our cold lunches. I watched Andy. After what I saw through the schoolhouse window, I suspected that he might be a bully. I was alarmed to see that he was slowly acquiring a 'following.' Norm Tucker was quickly becoming his sidekick. Norm was a year behind us in school but nearly our age. He missed being in our class because his birthday was two days after the cutoff.

"Hilda Barnum, you actually look like you're *trying* to be a girl!" Stella Johnson, my sister's best friend had a way of putting things that made your hair stand on end. "Can it be we are seeing a change this year?"

I had been sitting on the steps with Barb Bjornstad.

"Why, Stella?   Worried about some competition? Maybe you're a little jealous of the attention?" Barb shot back.

Stella snorted at this, "Jealous? Of Hildi Barnum?"

Stella turned on her heel and walked away. But I was stunned.

"What do you mean, Barb?"

She chuckled, "Hildi, you've got the boys noticing you."

I was about to respond when the bell rang.

Chapter Two

Most of us walked to and from school unless we had a storm. Stella's father always brought her and picked her up. Andy Porter complained about having to walk at all, even though his home was one of the nearest to the little school. But with his father at work and his mother still in town, there was no one to give him a ride. We didn't complain because we liked the walk.

"I don't like that new kid." Ben picked up a rock threw it as hard as he could after this statement.

Joe was next to him, "We have to love everybody, Ben. That's what Jesus said. 'Love your enemies.'"

Joe threw a rock, too.

"I know. I read it in the bathroom at home." Ben threw another rock.

Love Thy Enemies was a plaque in our bathroom and I had wondered why it was in there. It was part of a Bible verse. The rest was "... and pray for those who persecute you."

Lila was quiet.

"I think we should give him a chance," she said at last.

She was right. Maybe he just had to 'settle in' and get to know how we did things. We were automatically a bit prejudiced towards town-folk anyway. And I didn't appreciate being called a 'hick', especially in my own back yard!

Mom was sitting on the front porch with Grandma when we got home. They were slicing cucumbers and the smell of dill was thick. It was obvious to us that they had spent the day canning pickles. The grownups had spent the previous days at the Cooper farm helping them with their tobacco harvest. The cucumbers were beginning to rot on the vine, so it was no wonder that Mom and Grandma stayed home to get the pickling done.

"If you're hungry, go have a pickle." Mom said as we came up the steps. We could hear the pressure cooker in the kitchen.

"Oh, boy!" exclaimed Joe.

"Where are Granddad and Daddy?" I asked.

"They're over at Chet's helping get his tobacco in. Your dad wants to milk as soon as he gets home. There's a storm coming. Change your clothes and bring up the cows."

***

I squatted between two cows with a small bucket of dirty, soapy water. The barn was hot and the cows' sides heaved in and out in a near pant as they chewed their cuds. I wrung out the rag I used to wash the udders, as the cow lifted her hind leg next to me. I noted the deep wire-cut on the back teat and gently cleaned it. She put her foot back on the floor and even leaned into me a bit as I finished the washing part. She wasn't so forgiving when I took out the strip cup and squeezed several streams of milk into it from each quarter. I should have been ready for it, but she caught me by surprise as she quickly kicked out at me and knocked the strip cup out of my hand and into the gutter.

"Sooo," I said as soothingly as I could to a jersey cow. I tried to say it the same way my dad said it to settle them down, "so there, girl."

I picked up the strip cup, wiped it off, and glanced back at her bag. Rats! I was going to have to wash her again because in her effort to get rid of the annoyance--which was me--she'd left a big gob of manure on the cut teat. Once again I wrung out the rag, but this time I pushed my head into her flank right in front of the offending leg. When she lifted her hoof, I pushed even harder and was successful in keeping her from kicking me and I completed my task.

"Looks like that storm's gonna be here any minute." Even though it was early in the evening the barn was dark, the sun having been clouded over.

"Go on to the house, Hildi," Daddy said and I willingly obliged. Thunder had been rumbling since I went after the cows and now I could hear it over the sound of the milking machines.

Granddad stood in the doorway looking up at the sky. He was a big, square man whom I had held in awe my whole short life.

"Do you think it'll be a bad one?" I asked, looking up him.

He glanced back at me a moment and then back at the sky, "Sky's not green and the clouds don't look like cotton balls. I don't think we'll have a cyclone, but that don't mean we won't get washed away. There's a lot of lightning."

A gust of wind seemed to grow in the east and I could see the bluffs across the valley begin to fade as a wall of rain covered them and began to rush towards us.

"Better run, Hildi!" Granddad shouted over the sound of the oncoming storm.

I did and when I burst in the back door and into the kitchen, I wasn't too wet.

Boom! The thunder exploded overhead and made the glasses in the cupboard rattle. The lights in the kitchen flickered out. Mom had been peeling potatoes at the sink and she turned to look at who had just come in.

"Where are the boys?" she seemed worried.

They weren't with me. My ten year old twin brothers had their own chores. They had cleaned out the calf pens, thrown down more bedding, and fed the calves. After that they usually went to the creek or the pasture to play before supper.

"I don't know," was my answer and I could tell it wasn't what she wanted to hear.

By this time the lights had come back on and I could see the worry in Mother's face. She turned back to the sink and the window above it. Her eyes strained to see beyond the curtain of water that assaulted the earth below.

I knew what was coming and I was ready. I hadn't needed it earlier, but now I threw on a rain slicker and a pair of knee-high boots and charged back into the tempest just in time to be momentarily blinded by a flash of lightning and a deafening clap of thunder. Something in the pasture had been hit, a tree or maybe a cow, I didn't know. But I couldn't move as everywhere I looked, all I could see was the blue and white flash seared into my eyes. I rubbed them until I could see. Finally regaining enough of my senses, I raced to the pasture gate, ducked under, and headed for an area near the creek where the boys often played.

"Ben! Joe!" I called. The rain beat on my slicker making so much noise I could barely hear myself, let alone two boys answering back. But over and over I called, and on and on I searched until I saw the creek rising.

'Oh no! Dear God, please let them be all right!' I breathed the prayer as panic set in. I imagined the boys waiting until the last minute to head home and then trying to cross the swelling creek, being swept off their feet and falling under the water. Surely they were drowning.

"Hil---di--"

I stood still. Did I just hear my name? Was it the boys calling for help?

"Hildi!"

There it was again, but there was another sound with it. I held my hand up to my brow in order to keep the rain out of my eyes. There was something approaching. It looked like our Ford 9N tractor and it was coming as fast as it could. I ran towards it as it approached and when it stopped, I saw that it was Joe driving.

"Mom sent me to get you!" He yelled over the din.

My relief was mixed with anger at being on a wild goose chase, "Where were you?"

"In the hay mow stacking bales. Dad told us that when we got done with our chores, we had to 'burn off our energy' stacking the last load of bales."

I had heard that and kicked myself for forgetting. I went to the back of the tractor and stepped up onto the draw bar. I put a wet hand on each fender and Joe turned back towards the house.

"Electricity's off!" He hollered over his shoulder.

"You and Lila are supposed to go up in the attic and find the old kerosene lamps when we get back."

When we passed through the first pasture gate, Joe told me to shut it to keep the cows near the buildings. We didn't know how high the creek would get and if the cows would try to cross it. Daddy had told my brother that it was better to be safe and have all the cows close than to take a chance. Besides, flooding meant that the fences that crossed the creek would likely need repair. And if fences are down, cows are out.

Chapter Three

I was soaked through, despite my rain slicker and tall boots. Joe was, too and we were sent to the basement to change out of our wet clothes and dry off before being permitted into the kitchen or any other part of the house. Despite my earlier frustration, I thanked God that the boys were safe.

For the most part, our attic was off limits to us kids. I think this was to keep it neat and organized. Being snoopy, we would have gone through every box and trunk, exploring contents and probably not putting anything back until told. But we were also banned because Mom and Daddy hid our Christmas presents up there. These were not big items but mostly home-crafted things like clothes that Mom sewed and knitted while we were away at school. Daddy had built us girls a doll house and the boys a miniature barn and stored them up there years ago. So for Mom to send Lila and me upstairs into that treasure trove was like sending children to the candy store with a pocket full of change. I led the way, holding one of the two flashlights Daddy used for coon hunting.

The attic of our house was along the peak of the roof. A small door at the end of the hallway in the second story of our house led to a narrow stairway and that to the attic. It was dark, but Lila and I turned on Daddy's flashlight. The battery was giving out, so it was important that we find the old lamps as soon as we could.

"Where do you think they are?" Lila was behind me. Rain pounded the roof over our heads, but I felt safe and cozy in this space.

I shined the light around as best I could. Granddad had hooked the house up with electricity when he bought the farm twenty years earlier, even installing a single light in the attic. It hung near the center with a small chain switch. I pulled the chain and it clicked, but the bulb did not glow.

"Electricity's still out." I said and pulled the chain again to make sure the light would be off when the power came back on. "Mom said something about crates by the chimney."

We made our way in that direction and passed the frame of a 'Jenny Lind' bed, an old wooden barrel painted green with silver straps, a crib, a couple of stoneware jugs, crocks, and several boxes with unidentified contents. Near the chimney were two wooden crates without lids, and inside, wrapped in old newspapers, were the lamps with their tall glass chimneys. Lila stooped and lifted one which seemed to be quite large. She unwrapped it and discovered that it was ornately painted.

"Hildi, look at this!" The brass feet were tarnished and brown, but the glass which held the fuel was a beautiful green with a purple iris painted upon it. The over-sized globe top was also in the crate, carefully wrapped in newspaper and we lifted it out to fit it onto its base.

"Think of having your house lit up with something so beautiful!" she exclaimed.

I quickly noted the other crate with two less-ornate lamps and plain, clear glass chimneys.

Mom told us that there should be at least four lamps. We had found three. I shined the light around the chimney and saw a bundle of old newspapers tied up with a long piece of binder twine. The headline immediately caught my eye:

The Villain is Strung Up!

I pulled the bundle closer and knelt down. The date was October 26, 1897. The paper was nearly 50 years old and the article seemed to cover a good portion of the exposed page.

"Hildi, I'm taking this downstairs. Are you coming?"

I hadn't heard her. I was scanning the article. From what I could see, the paper was from the nearby city of Ridgeview, at that time called Ridge City.

"Hildi!" Lila's raised voice caught my attention. "What are you reading?"

"Something about a murder and a hanging. I want to read this," I never took my eyes off the paper. "I'll come in a minute."

"You have the light and it's going to go out. We won't be able to see enough to get out of here without tripping over something and breaking one of these lamps. Let's go!"

She had the crate with the fancy lamp and I lifted the other with the two, plain lamps. I had to hold the light and grip the crate, but what I really wanted was to bring that stack of papers, too.

We cautiously made our way down the steps and to the kitchen where Mom had lit a candle to help light the room. Ben was back from the barn by now, and Daddy had brought a can of kerosene in from the machine shed. We unwrapped the lamps and poured in a little kerosene. Mom showed us how to trim the wicks and then we lit them. The painted lamp stayed in the kitchen. She took the other two to our room and the boys' room.

"This is only three, girls. I want one in each bedroom."

"It's Hildi's fault." Lila complained.

Mom raised an eyebrow, "Why is that?"

"She was reading an old newspaper instead of looking for the other lamp."

Mom picked up the battery lantern and handed it to me, "Try to find that other lamp before this goes out. I don't want you having to take a flame up there. And instead of reading the old newspapers up there why don't you bring them down with you."

When I got back to the attic, I headed for the newspapers. I moved the bundle back to the attic steps and then began my search. I went back to where we had found the other lamps, but there were none there. I looked in various cardboard boxes only to find baby clothes, silk flowers, and packets of old cards that Grandma had saved. I went back to the chimney but this time moved boxes back until I was at the most acute slope of the roof, but I only found an old hat rack.

The battery in the lamp was nearly dead. I moved more boxes, found more 'junk'. I had nearly reached the other end of the attic. I discovered two old steamer trunks and looked inside but only saw old clothing folded neatly. In another box I found an old uniform.

At last the battery gave out and I was at the far end of the attic without making my discovery. There was a small window in the stairway and I eased myself along, hoping for enough light to find the door without tripping over anything. I suppose I should have been crawling and using my hands to feel for obstacles in my way, but I didn't have that much forethought. Suddenly, I tripped and fell with a great thud. I knew they heard me downstairs for Mom's voice carried up to see if I was all right.

"I'm fine!" I called back.

And when I sat up, my foot struck something that sounded like glass. I felt around with my hands, sticking them into boxes without seeing, hoping for no 'furry' surprises. At last it was the familiar feeling of something wrapped in newspaper which certainly seemed to be two more lamps with chimneys. This time, I stayed on all fours and carefully pulled the box with its breakable items with me to where I could see the faintest glimmer of light.

Managing the box and the newspapers would have been easy in daylight, but with no light on very narrow steps, it proved a bit treacherous. But I made it to the kitchen without any mishaps and once there, Mom and I unwrapped the last two lanterns only to find that one, another ornate lamp, had no chimney.

"I think lightning took out our power line." Daddy hollered in the back door, "It's either that or a tree is down on the line. Hildi, run down and close the gate so the cows can't get to the creek and that pole in the pasture."

"It's already done," Joe responded, "we got it just a little while ago."

I found a pair of scissors and cut the twine on the newspapers. Mom and Daddy continued their conversation while I carefully unfolded the topmost paper with the bold headline: The Villain is Strung Up!

The paper was from the Ridge City Clarion. The date was October of 1897. The biggest of the four lamps, the painted lamp with the large globe, sat in the middle of our kitchen table. Mom went back to preparing supper and I sat to read.

Who would have conceived a deed so dastardly to be committed by one of a family so esteemed in our fair Ridge City? None but the most imaginative might have dared to cast dispersions of this depth on a name so honored, but, alas, all this has been proven to be true!

Six days and one night previous the body of young Miss Mary Billings was found at the base of Lonesome Rock with several stab wounds to her body. So grim was the sight that even our brave Sheriff Llewellyn had to turn aside. Doctor Morsey was called in to make a report and it was discovered that the dear young girl had been in a dishonored state which the doctor believed may have been the reason for the attack. All hope of finding the fiend responsible for the butchery of this fallen child seemed lost until one night ago. Miss Lucinda Manchent, fiancé of young August Crenshaw, was discovered slain with a single bullet wound to her heart! Oh how the Great Judge of Humanity must be weeping to see such savagery in a town so untouched by lawlessness! A letter by Miss Billings' hand was found among Miss Manchent's affects, undiscovered by her assailant. In it, the poor dear confessed her soiled state and that it was indeed Mr. August Crenshaw who was responsible for bringing her to this dishonored position! This news soon spread and the community quickly formed a mob and marched upon the stately Crenshaw home. Young August must have known that the fates had determined the outcome, for he quickly took up a pistol and forced his devoted mother and sister from the home.

For several hours the rogue stood on the balcony as the good citizens of this community demanded his surrender. Shots were fired by both Crenshaw and one of the deputies, but none of them hit their mark. It finally came to an end at the dark hour of 1:14 a.m. this morning when the house fell silent. All feared that something was afoot and the door was finally battered down. And a grizzly sight it was that met the eyes of our fair citizens! August Crenshaw had taken his own life by hanging himself from the banister of the grand staircase! A letter, penned by his hand, was discovered on his body. It was clear that the brute was insane and he cursed the city, his family, his God and the very house where he died! Such a tragic end to three promising young lives!

I sat back in my chair, stunned by the crime, yet intrigued, as well. This happened just thirty miles away in a city I thought I knew. I wondered about the 'Crenshaws'. Ridgeview was an old city with ties to lumber and milling. There were several huge Victorian homes, but one in particular stuck out in my mind. Whereas most of these homes had been kept up as well as possible, some had fallen into disrepair.

"Whatcha got there?" Daddy looked over my shoulder.

I wondered how much he knew about this, "Daddy, is the Crenshaw house still standing or did something happen to it?"

His eyebrows shot up and he blew some air through his lips, "Where did that come from?"

I pointed to the headline and he bent over to read it.

"My goodness. Where did you find this?" He gently lifted the paper and turned its pages.

"It was up in the attic. I found a bundle of them tied together when we were looking for the lamps."

He stared at the paper while laying it back on the table and pulling up a chair.

"We used to hear stories about the old Crenshaw place when I was a kid and your Granddad was sheriff--like strange lights in the windows and low moans coming from inside. We used to dare each other to walk by the Crenshaw house on Halloween night. We'd get each other so scared that we couldn't sleep without lighting a lamp!

"That old house is still standing. It's made out of limestone, but it's in pretty bad shape. The truth is that the family that owned it, the family of the young man who died there, moved east after all this happened. The house was empty for about 10 years and then the family decided to sell it. But nobody would buy. Finally, they tried to make some apartments out of it and rented it out. During the Depression, things got so bad that there weren't any people who could pay the rent.

Eventually, it was completely abandoned. But here's where it gets really strange. I just heard that some outfit is renovating it from top to bottom. Someone bought it for the back taxes and plans on bringing it back to its former 'glory'. But there's something weird about that house. Folks still say it's haunted. And there have been some unusual accidents since those men started working on it."

By this time, Lila and the boys had gathered round to hear Daddy's story. Mom listened to this while she worked at the stove. Meatballs sizzled in the skillet and potatoes boiled in the pot, but when Daddy said the house was haunted, she turned and did not look pleased.

"Don't go putting those kinds of thoughts into their heads. There are no ghosts and houses cannot be haunted."

Dad smiled and I wondered if he had made the whole thing up just to get Mom's dander up. He did like to tease her!

"I'm sorry, hon. Your mother is right. There are no such things as ghosts. Let's talk about something else."

The talk turned to school and the new faces. Daddy said that Chet Cooper got all his tobacco speared and hung in the shed, the first in the valley to get his crop up.

"I'm afraid that wind is going to have ours all twisted or laying flat in the field. We should probably get it up before it rots," Mom said.

"Well, if that's what happens, that's what we'll have to do. At least we'll have help. Chet said that he and the boy will be over when we start on ours. I'll tell you one thing, those two can spear. And since Chet can't climb like he used to, Willie hung the peak. That boy's like a monkey. And strong! We had some big plants on those lathe and he handled them like a man."

"You sound like you're as proud of him as if he were your own son," Mom said over her shoulder.

Daddy shrugged, "I guess that ranch work was good for him, that's all."

Ben pulled a chair up next to our father, "That's all right, Daddy, we know you're proud of us, too."

My father smiled and ruffled Ben's hair, "That I am ... and you didn't even have to go to Montana."

Chapter Four

It was 5:00 a.m. when Mom opened our bedroom door, "Girls, get up quick! The cows are out in the corn and its going to take all of us to get them in!"

I had forgotten that the power had been out the night before, but it was back on now and we quickly threw on our overalls. No time for breakfast, because when cows get into the corn and over-eat, they could bloat and die. Queenie was our old cow dog and though she was very old and deaf, she still knew that she had a job to do.

Some of the cows were in the pasture bawling. They hadn't been with the escapees, so they didn't know where the break in the fence was. The cows in the corn were being stealthy. We fanned out and started down the rows, yelping and swinging sticks. Suddenly, there was a crashing sound. There are many sounds that a farm kid recognizes instantly and this was the sound of a dozen cows running for the gate with a nipping dog at their heels. Cornstalks bent and broke as the four-legged marauders tore through the field. Mom waited at the gate while the five of us and Queenie finished herding them out of the field.

"That went faster than I expected," she remarked.

But Daddy was kneeling by Queenie, "It would have been a lot longer if it hadn't been for this old girl." He rubbed her ears and petted her. But her eyes were tired and she panted harder than she should have. She lay down on her side and we watched her has she breathed hard.

"Is she all right?" Lila also knelt by the old dog and ran her hand gently over her head and back.

Daddy sighed, "She's old, Lila. She's way past retirement. We got this girl the year Hildi was born and that makes her pretty old to be chasing cows. I think one day we're going to go out to the barn and she will have just slept away."

At this Lila began to cry. These were quiet tears, not sobs. They rolled down her pretty cheeks and hung there only to drop off before she could wipe them away.

"Hey, sweetheart," Daddy said putting his arm around her shoulder, "Everything dies: people, cats, dogs, everything. It's part of nature."

She nodded, "Are you going to leave her here? Will she come up by herself?"

"No, I think ol' Queenie deserves to be carried today." So Daddy lifted the old dog in his arms and carried her home.

Chapter Five

Harvesting tobacco is back-breaking work. Not one bit of it can be done by a machine. The morning of the harvest the tobacco must be cut and laid down in rows. This means bending over, pushing the large plant back to expose the bottom of the stalk, and chopping it with a thin but wide-bladed axe as close to the ground as possible. If the axe isn't sharp, it might take several blows and one wrong move could mean stitches or the loss of a toe. These rows are left for an hour or more to wilt so that when the rows are put into piles the leaves don't break off. 'Pile rows' are comprised of five to seven rows of wilted plants. One tries to pick up as many plants as he can in each hand and carry them to the center row where the piles are made. If the plants are big, which you want, you can only carry two in each hand. By this time the sun is up and hot and it's not even noon yet. After the pile rows are made, the tobacco must be speared onto four-foot lathes. Big plants mean about five plants to a lathe. And when plants are speared, they sometimes fall off and have to be speared again, but in a different way so that they stay on the lathe. Sometimes the lathe breaks and then all the plants have to be put onto a new lathe. Eventually, it is noon and you can take a break for dinner which is good because you are probably sunburned and starting to ache. If the tobacco is especially pungent, your head might hurt. If you are wearing gloves, white canvas gloves which are lighter and thus cooler, the palms and fingers have turned black. After lunch you continue spearing. The crew splits in half and the other half begins hauling the speared plants to the tobacco shed to be hung and dried.

Tobacco sheds are around thirty feet tall and about the same width. Length varies. Our shed had six bents (a 'bent' is a section about twelve feet long) and each bent had about four sections reaching to the peak or top of the shed. A good harvest means you fill the shed to the peak and you hang the driveway. The haulers would drive through the field with a tractor or team of horses and a wagon and load the speared tobacco lathes onto the wagon. Once full, the wagon is pulled into the shed where it is unloaded. One man has to be on the wagon, and depending on how much room you need, you might have a man standing on each section up to the peak. You fill each level all the way to the floor, and if need be, you hang the driveway. But that was always a trick and always done last.

Did I mention that in the shed there are poles placed in order to hang the lathes of tobacco between? Our poles were never nailed down. If you were sure footed, you'd stand on the poles and balance and hope they didn't roll out from under you. If you were *me,* you demanded a plank to lay over the poles to have something more stable to stand on. If you were handing lathes of tobacco up to someone above you dirt and tobacco juice would fall back into your eyes and sting.

Around 3:00 you take your second lunch break which amounts to sandwiches, coffee, and pie. Then it's back to finishing up what is left in the field before chore time.

Miss Hendricks had taught in our area long enough to understand the importance of the tobacco harvest season to the farmer. Often our folks would pull us out of school to work until the harvest was complete. If the weather was good, we might only miss school on Friday and have the weekend to complete the harvest. Most folks in our area had less than four acres. We had two and a half.   The Cooper's had around that amount, but Gundersons had five. We all traded work back and forth, but we only got out of school for our own harvest. Saturdays were spent helping neighbors. Our moms, even though they also helped in the field, were happily excused to prepare the big meals we could only enjoy at harvest time.

We had been in school only a week when our own field of tobacco was ready to harvest. Daddy, Granddad, and Chet cut down several rows on a Thursday night and by 9:00 a.m. we were checking to see if it had wilted enough to pile. The storm had done some damage to our crop as far as twisting the stalks and making it difficult to cut. Other than that, the leaves were broad and in good shape. We spent that Friday working in the sun and getting burned. It was only our family, Granddad, and Chet. Grandma busied herself in the kitchen so Mom was able to be in the field. We piled plants until lunchtime, ate well, rested, and were back in the field spearing until 3:00. Chet went home at 4:30 as he had his own cows to tend. So we hauled tobacco without him. Daddy and Granddad and I climbed up onto the poles in the different sections. Mom was on the wagon and she passed lathes to me which I passed to Granddad and he passed to Daddy. We got to our own chores around 7:00 that night and supper wasn't until 8:00 or later. That was about a third of the harvest.

***

"How would you like to chop some tobacco this morning?" Daddy asked me at breakfast.

I knew that my eyes were as big as silver dollars. This was a big step up. You see, there is a kind of hierarchy to tobacco work. The top jobs were chopping and spearing. Kids and women, in general, did the piling. I don't include the hauling because when we had neighbors helping us, the men did the hauling, too. But when it's your family hauling, there's no great pleasure in it.

"Really? Yes!"

Daddy laughed "Ok, just don't let your axe slip and cut into your foot or your leg."

By 8:30, Daddy and I were back in the field. It was then that I learned that Granddad's sciatica was acting up, so he busied himself in other ways such as loading a wagon with bundles of tobacco lathe, making sure the tractor had fuel, and getting the shed ready for the loads of tobacco.

The sun was up, but the shadow of the bluffs covered that part of the field where we were and the plants were heavy with dew. The tobacco was tall, nearly four feet, and the giant leaves a good two feet long and another foot wide, so they held a lot of water. I started the walk to the field dry and warm and with a fresh pair of white canvas gloves, but once in the row and surrounded by the great plants, my gloves were soaked as well as my shoes. It wasn't long until the dew had soaked through my jeans up to my thighs. That would have been fine, but the leaves also contained that sticky juice that, added to the mixture, made one a bit uncomfortable.

"Make sure you're cutting as close to the ground as you can and that you cut it all the way through." Daddy reminded me.

He had a rhythm going and was far ahead of me. I stopped a moment, stood up from my stooped position, and watched him.

Step. Thwack! Step. Thwack! Went the sound of the stepping and the axe cutting through the stalks. And so on until he was flying through the row.

It took me the first row to find my own rhythm, but find it I did. I wasn't nearly as fast as Daddy and sometimes he would step over to my row and cut some of the plants ahead of me.

We had finished five rows when I heard more chopping behind me. Maybe it was Granddad or, perhaps, Mom had decided to join us. It was hard to see, for when you cut tobacco you walk bent over, looking at the plants to make sure you are accurate with your axe and hardly ever look up. Whoever it could be was moving fast and catching up to me.

I went back to my row, determined not to be passed. I gripped my axe tighter, but my gloves were wet and it was hard to maneuver with them on. I took them off and dropped them in the row as I went on. Now I could really fly.

"You dropped your gloves!" called a familiar voice.

But I didn't respond. I was almost at the end and I would win this race.

"Ha!" I shouted, completing my row and turning just in time to see Willie cut his last plant.

"Here," he said, handing me my gloves.

I was astonished. How could he stop to fish my gloves out of the row and still keep up with me?

I held out my hand to take the gloves, but when I did, I felt a sharp sting in the palm of the hand which held the axe.

"Oo!"

"That's what I mean," Willie took my hand in his and turned it over so I could see the huge blisters that had formed. "You're gonna get blisters anyway, but now they've opened up and you'll get that tobacco juice in them and they'll feel like they're on fire. Wear your gloves. You don't have to be a man."

Now, I knew what he meant. He wasn't putting me 'in my place'. He was just trying to tell me that I might not have the calluses of a man used to using his hands. But *I took it* as a challenge!

"For your information, I'm not *trying* to be a man!"

We both started down our rows heading for the next two. Daddy had already started his.

"What are you *trying* to be, then?" and that did sound like a challenge.

We were nearly back to where we started, "Faster than you!"

I bent and took off, but Willie was right beside me and within moments passed me. I tried to catch up, but as I picked up speed, I didn't cut all the way through the plants and had to chop more than once. This slowed me down more than when I wasn't trying to beat him. He finished long before me and waited at the end of the row.

"Maybe you need to sharpen that axe," he offered as I stood up and tried to work myself back into a normal standing position.

"Maybe *you* ... uh ..." I did not have a good enough response and left it there.

"Maybe you should go back to piling," he said and away he ran back to the other end to start his next row.

"Never!" I yelled and chased after him.

Thwack-thwack! Thwack-thwack, went our blades as we stooped and chopped. And each time he beat me. I would almost catch up and it was like he pushed a button and got a burst of speed that sent him faster and farther. And each time we would get to the end and race back to the beginning to start all over again. We were on our fifth row a-piece when I noticed that we were the only ones chopping. Daddy and Chet were sitting on the tailgate of Chet's Dodge truck.

"Wait a minute!" I was out of breath and we were at the point where we would have raced each other to the other end. "Do you see anything unusual down there?"

I pointed at our fathers with my axe.

"I think we've just been had!" exclaimed Willie who wasn't nearly as winded as me.

This time we walked to the end of the field and right up to the truck.

"You quittin' so soon?" Chet directed the question towards me.

"Yeah, you were doing so well!" added Daddy, "We thought you'd take the rest of the field down before 10:00!"

Willie laid his axe in the box of the truck and took off his gloves, "We didn't want you to miss out on all the fun."

The truck lifted when our dads dismounted from the tailgate. Taking their own axes, they picked up where we left off. They moved with the swiftness of veterans used to a task. We listened to the rhythm of the cutting as we sat silently where they had been earlier.

I took off my gloves and looked at the blisters on my right hand. They were broken and red with bits of dirt in them and they stung like everything.

"Let me see that." Willie sat to my left. As he reached across to take my right hand he leaned in close to me to have a look at the blisters. We were nearer each other than we had been since the night at the mill. And even though it made me uneasy, this was something I had longed for. I was afraid to breathe because I wanted it to last. But it only lasted a moment. Still holding my right hand, he hopped off the tailgate and came around in front of me.

"I stayed with my uncle Ethan in Montana. Well, he's got some stuff for blisters that makes 'em feel pretty good."

He talked lightly of his time on the ranch, all the while examining my blisters and carefully trying to pick out bits of dirt. I sat silently, while watching him. I suppose I stopped listening because I was caught up in my own thoughts. There were so many things I wondered and so much I wanted to say. He never wrote to me, but then, I hadn't written to him, either. I didn't understand my feelings and why they had changed and why I now thought about him *all the time*. He hadn't changed much since June. He might have been a little taller, his hair a bit lighter from hours in the sun, his voice a little lower, but he was still the boy I admired.

"I missed you." I said simply.

"Maybe some cow salve ..." he looked up at me. "... what?"

I was either all in or all out. It was just a statement. It was true. Did it matter if he knew it and shouldn't he know it anyway?

"I missed you." I said again.

And he just stood there, looking at me, holding my hand and saying nothing. Then, after what seemed like a good minute or more, the corners of his mouth turned up and his eyes softened. And when he spoke it was only two words nearly whispered.

"I know."

When Daddy hollered at us Willie dropped my hand and looked away.

"Like I said," Willie resumed what he thought was a casual tone but seemed to me to be strained, "you oughta put some cow salve on this. We've got a lot of work to do today, so you'd better see to it."

He reached back into the truck bed and picked up his axe before dashing off to the field.

I hopped off the tailgate and watched him. A lump jumped into my throat and I felt the familiar sting in my eyes, but I fought off the tears as I turned away. I had the overwhelming feeling that I'd said too much.

Instead of heading up to the house, I walked down the road to Grandma's. I knew that she would be there preparing food for the harvest crew. Granddad and Grandma's house was closer to the tobacco field than our own. But that's not why I went there. Mostly, I didn't want to talk to anyone.

"Hildi Barnum, didn't you wear your gloves?" Grandma scolded. She always scolded, so I guess I was used to it. But she was gentle as she dabbed balm onto my hand and carefully wrapped it. "This bandage will prob'bly work its way off when you get to piling or spearing."

It felt better and I said nothing.

"You wear those gloves." She chided. And then she seemed to stop short and gave me a sideways look, "There's something wrong."

I turned away quickly. I knew that the dam could break any moment and I didn't want to cry, but her warm hand on my back did just that and the tears flowed freely. I wiped my eyes and headed for the door.

"Hold on, now. I know you've been hurt worse than this and that's never made you cry. What's going on?" She was gruff, but I knew she didn't mean to be.

I shook my head and the tears streamed down my face.

"Sit down in that chair right there." She ordered me to one of the kitchen chairs by the table and wiped my face with a dish towel. "I'm not going to play a guessing game with you. Out with it. What is the matter?"

I took a deep breath, "I ... I told Willie I missed him ..." and I couldn't finish. It was strange, but when I told her the reason for my tears, it sure sounded stupid.

"What's wrong with that? I think we all missed the boy. Did he say something hurtful?"

I shook my head and Grandma sat down next to me. She stared at me for a moment and something changed in her eyes.

"Young love can be hard," she began, "it don't get much easier, Hildi. In fact, your heart may be broken more than once ... and you might break a heart or two yourself before it's all said and done."

I was stunned! Love? Is that what was happening?

She looked hard at me, "My word, yes, you've got it bad. Oh, it's probably just puppy love and it will pass, and you'll meet someone in a year or so and forget all about Willie Cooper."

"Grandma, Willie's my best friend! I don't want to forget about him!"

She smiled, "So what are you crying about? Get back down to that field and get busy!"

I felt better. I even smiled. Grandma gave me a cookie and I headed down the road. As I approached the field, I noticed that every row that had once stood tall was laid down and before I could reach it, Chet Cooper's green pickup was on its way back to our house with the men inside and Willie riding on the running board.

Chapter Six

When I got back to our house, I recognized my uncle's Plymouth and knew that my dad's older brother, Jerry, and his family had arrived. Jerry had a dairy farm in the county just south of ours and each year he brought his family to help us with the tobacco harvest. He was just as tall as Daddy, but thin like a rail. His wife, Ruth was short and round and one of the best cooks ever. Although they didn't raise tobacco, Ruth's side did which meant that my cousins knew all about harvest and were a big help. I knew that we would get our crop in when they showed up.

"I wondered where you were!" My uncle called from the doorway to our dairy barn. My dad and brothers were there, too, standing around and looking at something Jerry cradled in the crook of his arm. It was black and white and fuzzy. Queenie stood at his feet and wagged her tail as she looked up at whatever he held. It squirmed a little.

"Come over here," Daddy called.

As I drew nearer, I could see what all the commotion was about. That mysterious thing in my uncle's arms was a pup. It was asleep but stirred as Jerry gently held it out to me. I took the pup and held it against my chest, petting its silky fur and smelling the 'puppy' smell. It was soon awake and licking my face. The boys giggled and its little tail began to wag furiously.

Daddy spoke next, "Jerry's collie had pups a month and a half ago. This is the pick of the litter. She's a little honey, don't you think?"

My face hurt from the grin I wore. "She's really sweet!" I exclaimed.

"Well, she's yours," said my uncle, "that is, she belongs to all of you."

"Really?" We had just talked about poor old Queenie needing to retire, but that had just been a few days earlier.

Daddy nodded, "I knew Jerry's dog was going to have pups and had asked for one before they were born. We've just been waiting until they were old enough to be separated from their mother."

"And she's a great cow dog, real smart and quick. This little lady should be a lot like her." Jerry offered, "Hey Matt, you said she was a little 'honey'. Maybe that should be her name."

"I like it." said Ben.

"Me, too," Joe added.

"Then 'Honey' it will be." Daddy declared.

Jerry and Daddy began talking of the upcoming fishing trip. This was something they always talked about, but never did. However, this year it looked like it would happen. Jerry had made reservations at a cabin up north and Daddy, Chet, and Granddad had begun cleaning up their old tackle. Granddad had an old fishing boat and over the summer had gone through it, making sure that it was 'sea worthy'. The plan was to be carried out the last weekend in September if everything worked out.

As the men continued their plans, my cousins emerged from the house. They were three stout boys with the youngest being about my age. All three were dark-haired with green eyes. It appeared that only the youngest would be tall like his father, the other two being short and round like Ruth.

"Where've ya been?" Arnie, the oldest, cried.

Harry took a closer look at me before saying anything. He was the youngest. "You been up to Granny's."

"She'll swat you if you call her 'Granny' to her face!" Ralph, the middle cousin gave his brother a shove and he tripped forward into me.

Jerry swiftly stepped between the two who appeared to be ready to take each other to the ground. He grabbed one in each arm and held them while they tried to wriggle free.

"I'm not puttin' up with this today, boys! You'll settle down and behave or you'll spend the day piling without ever touching a spear or climbing in that shed!"

This was great entertainment for us. I always liked it when the boys were around. They were hard workers, but there was always a bit of competition between them which eventually led to some kind of fight or wrestling match before the day was out. But it was all in good fun. No blood was ever spilled and nothing ever bruised except for an ego.

"I think we'll be ready to start piling in about half an hour. Hildi and I started cutting around 8:30 and the sun's been on those rows for quite a while. We'll let it get a good wilt and then we can get going." Daddy relieved me of the pup and handed it to Ben and Joe who both petted her and put her in the barn. Queenie followed, all the while wagging her tail slowly.

Thanks to the puppy and the excitement of the cousins, I had quite forgotten why I'd gone to see Grandma. But then I heard the engine of Chet's truck and saw it slowly pulling out of the yard and heading down our driveway.

"Where are they going?" I asked.

"They're going home for a while, but they'll be back this afternoon. Chet's got some work to do and the girls want to come too." I felt Daddy's big hand on my shoulder, "Did you get some blisters?"

I held up my hand so he could see the bandage Grandma put on it.

"Uff Da!" exclaimed Jerry, "Broke open, did they?"

I nodded, but kept my eye on the truck as it disappeared down the driveway.

"Let's go have some coffee and donuts," Daddy headed towards the house and we followed.

***

There were nine of us who went to the field to pile, and we got it all done by dinner time. Now, on the farm, dinner was at noon and supper at night. Lunch came after dinner around 3:00

and consisted of sandwiches and desserts. But dinner ... oh my! With Mom, Grandma, and Aunt Ruth all cooking, we had quite a feast. There were two roasts, meatballs, potatoes and gravy, rolls, baked beans, cabbage salad, pickles, jello salad, and so much more. There were pies: apple, cherry and blueberry and chocolate cake! No one thought about diets. We spread home-made butter on our bread, drank whole milk, and ate sliced cheese. We knew that in an hour we would be back to work, burning up all the fuel we'd just taken in. But before that, we rested a little under the big spreading elm trees in our yard. It had turned into a good, hot day and the sky was a deep blue you only see in August. Every so often a breeze would carry the light aroma of tobacco from the field to us. This was a different odor than the way the tobacco smelled when you're standing in the field with the sun was beating down on it. This was pleasant.

"Hildi, come in and help with the dishes," my aunt Ruth called from the porch.

I reluctantly got up from the carpet of soft grass and met the feminine portion of the harvest crew in the kitchen.

"Do you take the paper?" asked Ruth.

"We do," answered Grandma.

"Did you read that article on the old Crenshaw house, Grammy?" I always thought it strange that Ruth called her mother-in-law 'grammy'. 'Mother Barnum' or 'Mom Barnum' would have made more sense to me. They stood at our kitchen sink as Mom washed the dishes and Ruth and Grandma Barnum covered the leftover food with tinfoil and put it in our refrigerator. I dried the dishes and Lila put them away. We both knew, if we looked like we were busy and not paying attention, our elders would speak more freely and we might learn something.

"I did. If you ask me, somebody should have put a match to that house long ago." Grandma didn't even look up when she spoke.

But Aunt Ruth persisted, "Oh, Grammy, it's just a building."

At this point Mom became interested, "What was in the article?"

"Oh just some strange goin's on, that's all. Hershel Dobkins bought it for the back taxes. The paper said some local construction company…"

"Porter Construction," Grandma remarked.

Ruth continued, "…that's right, Porter Construction is who he hired to fix it up. Says he's going to make it a fancy hotel for some rich characters from Chicago who like to come up here and fish trout in Ottertail creek. But…"

She seemed to pause for dramatic effect, "The owner of the company has had some trouble with stolen tools and some strange accidents. One of his men fell off some scaffolding and broke his leg pretty bad. Then they had a fire in some old lumber they'd torn out and had sittin' in a pile. None o' that probably would have made anybody look twice. But when this Porter started having some strange things happen at his home ..."

"Porter ..." Mom looked at me, "that Porter boy at school, did you say his dad is in construction?"

"That's what he said," Lila answered before I could.

"That's not this Porter. The one I'm talking about is from Ridgeview," Ruth remarked shortly. She figured she knew more than us.

But I jumped in, "I think it is. He said they were from Ridgeview."

"Well, now, Hildi Barnum, you might very well be right. Anyway, they haven't been around this area long. They moved here from the eastern part of the state." Aunt Ruth did not look pleased, like I had taken something away from her exclusive story. Now she added this last bit of information to make sure she still knew more than me.

"What kind of strange things?" Lila insisted our aunt continue with the story.

"Well now, flat tires on a car parked in a garage, telephone lines going dead, then strange sounds in their basement ..."

Grandma stopped and addressed Ruth, "That was not in the article. None of that was in the paper!"

Ruth put her hands on her ample hips, "I know that, Grammy. I heard it from Beulah Perkins. Beulah's sister's brother-in-law works for this Porter and he told her and she told me."

Grandma's mouth was a straight line. Aunt Ruth was the family gossip and we got all the dirt there was to hear when she was around. We girls loved it, but Mom and Grandma never seemed to appreciate the information.

***

We hauled tobacco on two different wagons. One person drove the hay wagon and we laid the lathes of tobacco flat in piles on both sides. In this way, we were able to load two rows at a time. Then we had a 'tobacco' wagon. This had two eight-foot long four by fours that stood up about six feet with two by fours on top that ran the length of the wagon. Instead of laying the lathe flat on the wagon, they were hung between the two by fours.

By the time we'd finished 'gossiping', the men and boys had already left, so the four of us walked to the field and visited as we went. This was one of the few times that I saw my grandma not wearing a dress. Just as we got to the field, the Cooper truck pulled up. Chet and Julia, Willie's folks, were in the front and his sisters, Kathy and Betty, were in the back. But I didn't see Willie anywhere.

"Hello there!" Mom called.

"Do you think we'll get all this in today?" Julia adjusted the scarf on her head.

"I sure hope so. Did you bring spears?"

The tobacco spears fit over one end of the lathe allowing one to 'spear' the tobacco onto the lathe. Chet held them up. But I was busy looking around. I still didn't see Willie.

Kathy was pulling on a pair of well-worn canvas gloves over her engagement ring. She took a step towards me as she followed my gaze.

"If you're looking for my brother, it might be a while," she said and pulled a large-brimmed straw hat out of the front of the truck.

"Where is he?" Lila asked. But Betty stepped between Kathy and me.

"Did you have a quiet summer, Hildi?" she asked and not so subtly began to lead me towards the field, but Kathy followed us.

"He's at home, reading a letter from *Ramona*."

She had our full attention now and I felt the hair on the back of my neck stand up.

"Ramona?" I asked.

My sister Lila used to be as shallow and spiteful as Kathy. But Lila had changed, for the most part. On the other hand, Kathy had gotten worse and I couldn't figure it out.

"Just some pretty little thing he met when he was in Montana. And every Saturday since he's been home, he gets a thick letter from her. She even sent some pictures of her and Willie on horseback."

My mouth went dry and my heart felt like it would burst. So ... that was the difference. Betty gave her sister a glare that either Kathy missed or she ignored.

"C'mon, Hildi. Let's get busy."

I was never one to chase after a boy. I suppose there had never been a 'need' to do that and I wasn't going to chase Willie. He had been my best friend my whole life. But, even though I was young I realized that sometimes 'life' disappoints you. Life goes on. When he did finally show up, I made no attempt to talk to him. I busied myself and avoided him.

***

We did get all our tobacco in that Saturday, but it wasn't easy. Jerry and Ruth had to leave by 4:00 in order to get home and get their cows milked. Coopers left at around 5:30. Granddad and Grandma did the chores while the rest of us loaded and hauled the speared tobacco. By 9:00 we had brought up the last two loads and hung the lathes in the shed by tractor light.

We were all worn out. Every muscle ached and we all had sun burned skin. Our faces were smudged from dirt and our clothing stiff and grimy from the hard work. And by the time we got the last of the big plants speared, they'd taken on the pungent, sickening aroma that smells like dirty, moldy laundry. It stuck in our nostrils. But we were glad to be done with this portion of the harvest. And better yet, we didn't have to go to the barn that night.

"I think I'll just lie down on the living room floor," Ben groaned and did just that. His brother joined him in front of the fireplace.

With the sun down, there was a chill in the air, so Daddy stepped over them and lit a fire. The wood smoke was a nice change and the heat felt good in spite of our burned skin.

"Any pie left?" he asked, collapsing onto the couch beside Mom.

"If you want any you'll have to get it yourself." Mom leaned her head against the back of the couch and shut her eyes.

Lila came in last but had something with her. It was Honey. Her little paws made scratching noises on the wood floor.

"You know we don't let dogs in the house," Mom reminded her.

But Daddy was quick to come to Honey's defense. He picked up the pup and set her in his lap, "It won't hurt to let her stay in for a little bit."

Mom petted the soft fur and was rewarded with a wet puppy kiss, "Just don't make it a habit. After all, how do you think this makes Queenie feel?"

Ben rolled onto his side, "If I wasn't so tired I'd let her in, too, so she wouldn't get her feelings hurt."

Mom let out an exasperated sigh, "I'm taking my bath. I don't care if I use up all the hot water."

Daddy wrapped his arms around her, "Maybe I should come up with you ... maybe we could conserve some water."

Mom's eyes grew wide as she pushed him away, but not too hard, "Matthew! What will these kids think?"

But Mom had a light in her eyes and Daddy kissed her on the cheek.

"Put Honey back in the barn and shut the door," she said, getting up and heading for the open stairway. "Remember we've got church tomorrow."

The rest of us, including Daddy, sat in front of the fire for a long time, petting Honey and being quiet with our own thoughts. We all had our turn in the bathroom and Daddy promised to put a shower in the basement when we complained that the hot water wouldn't last. I was last to take my bath and the hot water was nearly gone. When I finally crawled under the covers, I was ready for sleep, except for the thought that continued to trouble me.

"Hildi?"

Lila was still awake.

"What?"

"What are you thinking about?"

I took a breath and confided, "I don't own Willie Cooper. He's not my boyfriend, so I shouldn't be upset if he's getting letters from a girl named Ramona."

I heard her turn over, "Hildi, just because he's getting letters from her doesn't mean he's writing back."

Chapter Seven

Our little country church was always full. It drew folks from miles around. There were many more kids who lived just outside our school district that we never got to see except on Sunday. So we looked forward to Sunday, not just as a day of worshipping the Lord, but also as a time to see people we didn't get to see anywhere else.

We averaged around seven kids in our Sunday school class that were all within a year or two of each other in age. But on this Sunday, there were only four of us: Lila, myself, George Lowry, and Virginia Jessup. The preacher's wife taught our class and always wore a smile. The deep creases around her eyes were evidence of her sunny disposition. She was a heavy-set woman with silver hair and gold wire-rimmed spectacles. Her hands were beefy and looked soft as she turned the pages of her well-worn Bible.

"Well, let's see how many of you remember last week's lesson. Anyone?"

Lila raised her hand.

"Go ahead, Lila," encouraged the pastor's wife.

"It was about charity and that charity means love and in some Bibles it says 'love' instead of 'charity'. "

She nodded, smiling all the while, "Do you remember anything else or can someone add to what Lila said?"

Our classroom was right under the stairway that led to the basement and I could hear someone coming slowly down the steps.

George lived on the other side of Ottertail creek, "It was from Corinthians. And Paul wrote Corinthians."

The curtain was pulled aside and in walked Willie. The Coopers were always late on Sundays, but they always came.

"Good morning, William Cooper!" Mrs. Potter welcomed, "It is so good to see you! You are looking quite well. We were just reviewing last week's lesson."

He looked around the long table with all the empty seats. Mrs. Potter, the Pastor's wife sat at the head of the table with Lila and me next to each other on one side and George and Virginia on the other. He pulled out a chair next to Virginia and sat down right across the table from me. I didn't look up at him but stared at my Bible. I kept my hands in my lap, hiding the hand that Willie had held the previous day.

"We are in First Corinthians, chapter thirteen. Do you remember anything about this chapter?"

Willie quickly found the book and the chapter and spoke as he turned the pages, "It's known as the 'Love chapter'."

"Well done!" said Mrs. Potter, "Anything else?"

"You hear this chapter at a lot of weddings, but it's not about that kind of love. It's about Christians loving the Lord and each other. You can die for the Lord, but if you don't love Him completely, your sacrifice is for the wrong reason."

Selma Potter took off her glasses, "That's right. I take it you didn't neglect your Bible when you were in Montana."

I looked up in time to see his warm smile. It made me wonder.

Chapter Eight

"What I did on my summer vacation."

It was the day I dreaded ... the day Miss Hendricks passed back our themes. She walked slowly up and down the rows of the fourth through eighth grades and handed back our papers. I dreaded getting mine back. Oh, eventually I came up with something, but it was not up to scrub. She finally placed mine on my desk in front of me. The C+ was not exactly a surprise. But the note under it made me want to crawl under my desk.

Not quite up to your usual level of work.

Miss Hendricks did not call on me to read my theme this time. But Willie read his. We all learned about the Rawlins Ranch in the Bitter Root Mountains of Montana. He told us about all the 'cowboy' stuff he did like riding, branding, and roping. He'd been to a real ghost town called Virginia City and had seen a mountain lion and a grizzly bear. Finally, he said he'd made new friends and he wanted to go back one day.

Several other students also read their themes. Lila was one. She disappointed some of the kids by not writing about shooting Emmit Romney at the old Weston Mill. Instead, she reported on summer camp and farm work. Others told about trout fishing, killing a rattlesnake, doctoring sick animals, swimming and fishing in the Mississippi River. But it was Andy Porter's paper that held our attention.

"What I did on my summer vacation: A man named Hershel Dobkins hired my father's construction company to restore the Crenshaw house in Ridgeview. Up until the last few weeks, that was where we lived, in Ridgeview, not in the Crenshaw house. The Crenshaw house is solid limestone and my father says it is structurally sound. It's been unoccupied for the last thirteen years or so. Fifty years ago, a man named August Crenshaw killed two women. When the town found out he was the one who killed them, they took out after him. He ended up hanging himself in the house before he could be arrested and probably lynched. Some folks told my father that if he went to work on the house, bad things would happen because the house is cursed.

"My brothers and I don't usually get to help my dad at work, but since it was summer and we needed to make some money, he let us work with him a few hours each week. The first couple of weeks went pretty smooth. But in July we had our first accident. We rigged up some planking over the stairway in order to set up a ladder and reach the old chandelier in the entryway. The planking consisted of brand new boards that were easily two inches thick. One of my father's workers stepped up onto the ladder and the planking gave way. He broke his leg in two places. The boards were inspected as well as the ladder and the stairway itself. There was no reason for them giving out.

"A week later, we had our second accident. We were in the process of ripping out the old lathe and plaster and hauling the wood outside. We had quite a pile and had planned on loading it up over the weekend and hauling it to the dump. That night we had rain and it soaked the pile. The next morning when we came to work, it was on fire, a fire so big we had to call the fire department.

"There were other incidents: electric saws starting on their own, strange howls coming from the cellar. Every time we tried to explain it or find a source for the sounds, we came up empty. My Dad says that people are starting to give him strange looks, like, 'there's that crazy guy who's workin' on the cursed house.'

"Then there were the strange messages left in the sawdust on the floor: Leave! Get out now! Cursed! But the worst was when my father went to close up the house for the night and on his way out the front door, he looked back at the stairway to see a noose hanging from the railing! After that, he decided we needed to get out of town, so that's why we're renting the Oliver place.

"Maybe the Crenshaw house is haunted. Maybe Dobkins has an enemy and doesn't want him to fix up this place. I don't know. What I can tell you I just did. What I can't tell you is why we're here and why my old man keeps working on that house, especially when his crew refuses to go near it."

We all stared at Andy and he stared straight ahead. Was this real? I couldn't tell if he was putting on or not, but the room was dead silent. Miss Hendricks had read his theme so she knew what was in it. But even she looked dazed.

"Thank you, Andy. I don't remember all of that being in your theme." She remarked.

"But it's true. I decided to tell it all. I don't care."

Miss Hendricks looked concerned, "You may sit down, now. I think we've heard enough for today. It's time to do some arithmetic."

****

It was a few days later. Lila was poised at home plate as she rested the bat on her right shoulder and squinted at the pitcher. We were down by three in the last inning with the bases loaded and two outs. It was 'do or die' and I was at third ready to lead off with the next pitch. The pitcher wound up and let fly with a fast under-handed stinger. Lila swung hard and everyone could hear her when she grunted with the effort.

"Strike one!" Hollered Shorty Shimshack who was in sixth grade.

Lila turned just long enough to glare at the near-sighted umpire.

"C'mon, Lila!" I called from my post at third. "Bring me home!"

My brothers, Ben and Joe, laughed from behind second base and right field. They knew that Lila's hitting record at our noon softball games wasn't good. She *always* struck out. Oh, she looked good at bat. In fact, she appeared very athletic, even in her feminine blouse and skirt. But she was never quite able to connect bat to ball. Nevertheless, I was determined to encourage a hit out of her before the game was over.

The pitcher smiled but didn't tease. He looked over his shoulder at me as I thought about stealing home. I'd only taken a step off the base but he gave me a knowing look; and I put my foot back where it belonged, then he turned back to the batter.

He wound up again and the ball left his hand like lightning.

"Strike two!" Shorty called.

Lila hadn't even had time to swing. She let the business end of the bat fall to the ground with the call and looked dejected.

"Why don't you throw something she can swing at!" Norm Tucker was on our team, but not usually on *our side*. He was a good hitter, but the pitcher, Willie, had struck him out first. Now Norm was sore. He didn't like losing, even in a recess game.

Willie stood up straight and looked hard at Lila.

"You ready?" he asked her. I could see her take a deep breath and lift the bat back up to her shoulder.

She nodded, but Willie didn't wind up. Instead, he walked to home plate and right up to Lila.

"What're you doin', Cooper?" yelled Andy Porter. He was covering me at third, so he was plenty loud. He continued to grumble under his breath, even uttering some words we rarely heard at our country school.

I watched as Willie took Lila's hands and moved them up the bat a few inches. Then he said something to her and I could see her nod. It was only a few moments but soon Willie was striding back to the pitcher's mound.

"Remember what I said. Keep your eye on the ball."

Lila gripped the bat, widened her stance, and leaned over home plate. Willie wound up and sent the ball flying. I could see the determined look on my sister's face and for a moment I felt sorry for her. I would soon be walking in with the rest of our team as I anticipated the strike.

"Crack" went the bat. She hit it! She actually hit it! And this wasn't just a base hit! Oh no! That ball was sailing into the outfield where my brother Joe had been daydreaming and came down somewhere behind him where it bounced into the cornfield that bordered the school grounds.

"Run!" someone yelled, "Hildi! Run home!"

I had been standing there stupidly watching the ball until the order brought me to my senses. I crossed home plate at top speed and watched as the others, with Lila last, followed me in.

"One, two, three, four! Four to three! We win!!" Norm hollered.

Well, we could only play three innings at our noon recess.

The bell rang and broke up our little celebration. Willie jogged in and I watched with admiration.   All that my sister needed was coaching ... but then, I had tried time and again to help her. I guess all she needed was the 'right' coach.

"Thanks, Will!"   Lila hugged Willie quickly and ran inside.

"Where's the ball?" Norm called, "We've gotta find that ball! It's my big brother's and if I don't bring it home ..."

"Quit-yer whinin'!" Andy said and headed toward the cornfield behind Norm.

We climbed the steps while Miss Hendricks watched the two behind us head in the opposite direction, "Where are they going?"

"Lila hit a home run and Norm's gotta find his brother's baseball."

She looked at the watch broach on her dress, "You have five minutes, boys!"

Andy waved to acknowledge that he'd heard her.

We found our seats and took out our books for the next lesson. But five minutes stretched into ten and then fifteen. Miss Hendricks was becoming irritated. We could all see it in the way she held her mouth.

"Ben Barnum, go see what's keeping those boys."

My little brother obeyed and was gone another five minutes. When he returned his face was red. He gestured to her to come near. When she did he whispered in her ear and her face grew red, too. She disappeared out the door and he took his seat.

"What's goin' on? Where are they? Where's Miss Hendricks going?" Questions came from around the room and Ben turned to answer.

"They were smokin' cigarettes and they looked pretty mad when they saw me. I ran back here as fast as I could."

"Smokin' in the cornfield? Did they find the ball?"

He nodded but he seemed frightened.

Soon, Miss Hendricks was back with the two offenders. Both boys gave Ben a look that said 'you're dead' as they passed him to take their seats. I had the urge to stand up for my brother, but I controlled my temper.

Whenever Willie got in trouble, his punishment consisted of staying an extra hour after school and splitting wood and then getting his hide tanned once he got home. Norm knew what to expect, but I wondered how Andy would take his punishment.

I didn't have to wait long to see Andy's retribution towards my brother. I was busy trying to figure the square root of 14,684 when I heard a crash behind me and turned in time to see Ben laying spread eagle between the rows of desks. He was up on his elbows in an instant and shook his head. At that moment, Andy leaned over and I clearly heard him whisper, "That's just the beginning!"

Before I could get on my feet Miss Hendricks was passing my desk.

"Take your seat, Ben." She kept her back to me but I could imagine her eyes drilling into Andy. "Stand up."

All eyes were on the new boy. He slouched in his desk, refusing to meet her gaze. She waited and he looked uneasy. He raised his eyes just long enough to scan the room. Everyone stared at him.

"What?" he growled.

"Stand up." She repeated slowly, never raising her voice.

He stirred and finally complied. She turned and walked to the front of the room then gestured for him to follow. He did, shuffling his feet as casually as he could.

She opened the cupboard behind her desk and reached inside producing a large wooden paddle.

"Grab your ankles, Andy."

He shook his head incredulously. We knew what was coming despite the fact that Miss Hendricks rarely had to resort to spanking anyone.

"What?" he said again, "Is this how you hicks do things? A kid trips over his own big feet and you blame the new kid? Nice!"

"Quit lyin', Andy." It was Willie, "I watched you trip him and I heard what you said. Take your punishment."

The new boy's eyes were locked with Willie's and neither one blinked. His jaw jutted out in defiance.

"That will do, William," Miss Hendricks did not appreciate Willie's help. "I'll tell you again, Andy, grab your ankles."

With a sneer he did and she gave his backside three quick, hard slaps with the board. She never gave more than three and never less.

Now it was Andy who was red-faced when he walked slowly back to his desk, but I felt this was not over.

Chapter Nine

"Cigarettes?" Daddy shook his head and looked at Granddad from between two cows.

Granddad laughed, and so did Daddy.

"What's so funny?"

Granddad gestured at my father, "There was a time when he got caught smoking corn-silk behind the outhouse. First he got a lickin' at school and then another when he got home. Boy was your grandma mad!"

"She broke her wooden spoon on my bottom!"

But I wasn't amused, "Go ahead and laugh. I'm worried about Ben."

"Ah! Bullies have to be put in their place. He was probably just blowin' off steam. Chances are now that he's had some of the wind knocked out of his sails that he'll settle down."

But I didn't think so. I had seen something in Andy Porter's eyes that told a different story.

***

The very next day Andy was true to his word. The tormenting began as soon as we arrived at school and Norm Tucker was the deliverer.

"Good morning, Hildi. Good morning, Lila. Good morning, Joe. Good morning, *snitch*!"

I was back in overalls. I knew I wouldn't be able to stand dresses more than a week or so. That being the case, I was ready for battle and stepped right up into Norm's face. "Would you like to say that again?"

Usually, Norm would back down but today he didn't. "Your brother is a dirty little snitch, a tattle tale!"

"And you're turning into as big a bully as Andy Porter!"

Norm took his index finger and gave my shoulder a poke. I gave him a shove and Lila was right next to me.

"Stop it, Hildi!" Ben shouted. Joe was beside his brother. "I can handle it."

I didn't move. If you've ever seen two tomcats square off with their tails swishing back and forth and their eyes not wavering, that was Norm and me.

"Take it back!" I ordered.

"Hildi!" It was Ben again. "I mean it!"

I looked at him and his face was stone. I knew in an instant that I had overstepped.

"What's this?" Behind me I heard Andy Porter's mocking voice, "You gotta get your big sister to fight for you?"

Ben's expression said it all, *'Why can't you stay out of it?'*

That morning I backed off, but I was observant the rest of that day. Ben took a good deal of abuse, not out and out violence or torture, but lots of little things that he tried to take in stride. His pencil box went missing during morning recess. At lunch, he opened his bucket only to find it empty. We shared our sandwiches with him, but I kept my eyes on Andy and Norm who were very amused at our mother 'forgetting' to pack Ben's lunch. Joe was clearly losing patience with this whole thing.

When Miss Hendricks rang the bell, we returned to the schoolhouse. There had been no noon baseball game. We had been watching dark clouds gathering in the west. Rain was coming and we were in a hurry to get back in. Several of us girls had been sitting together and hurried up the steps when we heard a commotion behind us. We turned in time to see someone lying at the bottom of the steps. Ben was face down on the ground and looked hurt. I raced down the steps as Andy stood over him, leering.

"Now we're even!" he spat.

But Joe had seen and heard enough. He threw himself at Andy who was more than a head taller. "You hurt my brother!"

Ben's nose was gushing blood. I searched for something to soak it up.

None of Joe's blows seemed to connect and all he did was wear himself out. Miss Hendricks was at the foot of the steps before anyone knew it. Willie grabbed Joe and pulled him off Andy. Lila and I helped Ben up and made our way to the pump where we started to clean him up.

"What in heaven's name happened?" Miss Hendricks was angry when she addressed Andy. "Did you punch him in the nose?"

"I'm telling you the truth, Miss Hendricks, he tripped and hit his nose on the railing there. Ask him."

I shook my head.

"You expect me to believe that?" She asked.

But Andy was insistent, "You ask him."

There were tears streaming down Ben's cheeks. Lila had found a rag, soaked it in the icy well water, and held it to the bridge of his nose.

"Ben, you tell me the truth now," started Miss Hendricks, kneeling in front of my brother and looking intently at him. "Did you trip or did someone hit you?"

Ben was visibly shaking. "I ... I tripped."

Miss Hendricks looked disappointed and waited for him to change his statement. When he didn't, she stood up and looked hard at both Andy and Norm. I noticed Willie had positioned himself between Joe and the other two. Our teacher moved closer to Ben, taking the rag from Lila and looking at Ben's nose and into his eyes.

"Hildi, I want you to walk Ben home. It could be that his nose is broken. I'll bet it is and he'll probably have two black eyes to boot."

We could see that his nose was swelling and there was a nasty purple bruise beginning to form across the bridge.

She addressed the students who still stood around. "The rest of you quit gawking and get back to your seats." She began shooing the younger students back inside. I nodded for Lila and Joe to follow.

I noticed both Norm and Andy snickering. So did Willie. When they moved to go inside,

Willie stepped in front of them. "Leave Ben alone."

"Butt out, Cooper!" Norm warned.

Willie ignored him, "Listen, Andy, you're new here, and maybe they do things different in Ridgeview. But around here, we don't put up with bullies."

"That a threat? 'Cause if it is, why don't you back it up?"

Willie backed towards the steps. "Not now."

He turned and went inside.

Andy chuckled and shook his head, "Chicken!"

I knew better.

As soon as we got home and Mom had a look at Ben's nose, she loaded us both up and headed for town. She dropped me off at school before continuing on to see Doctor Briggs. Later, when Lila, Joe, and I got home, we found Ben lying on the living room couch with a towel full of crushed ice on his face.

"Well," Mom began, "it's broken. Doc Briggs said that there isn't much to do for it except give him an aspirin for the pain and try to control the swelling."

Daddy sat at the kitchen table as they talked.

Joe picked up Ben's feet and sat down under them, gently placing them on his lap.

Lila and I sat on the floor. Ben lifted the ice bag and revealed his swollen nose and a pair of black eyes that hadn't been there before.

"Oh, Ben!" cried Lila. "Does it hurt much?"

He nodded and shut his eyes while placing the ice bag on his nose and forehead. She looked at me with tears in her eyes and then back at Ben. Joe rubbed his brother's stocking feet.

"I really wanna punch those guys! None of this woulda happened if that Andy hadn't moved here!"

I sat silently thinking that very thing to myself. I really wanted to blame Norm and Andy. But maybe they were telling the truth. Maybe Ben really had tripped. But that didn't explain why Andy had said they were 'even.'

"I'll do your chores, Ben." Joe said. "I'll do 'em for the next couple days."

"Thanks." Ben's voice was muffled under the ice pack.

"And Mom said you'll be staying home from school tomorrow, so I'll help you with your homework."

"Thanks," my brother repeated.

A voice from the other room called in, "Joe, go bring up the cows."

Joe picked up his brother's feet and got up off the couch. Lila also got up and went upstairs to change. But I remained.

"Ben."

"Mm?" he groaned.

"Look at me." I waited for him to take the ice pack off again. He looked miserable. "I want you to be honest with me. I promise I won't tell Mom and Dad and I won't tell Miss Hendricks."

"I already told you," he began, "I tripped."

"Over Andy Porter's foot?"

He looked away.

"Did he trip you?"

He nodded and placed the ice pack over his nose.

Chapter Ten

It was late September and we had already been in school a month. Ben's nose had healed, but now had a bump on its bridge. Miss Hendricks seemed to be on edge. I blamed the bully, Andy Porter.

I watched Willie from afar. He was truly the bravest boy I knew. I had seen him tackle an armed man nearly twice his size. I'd seen him fight for me. But now he wouldn't fight for himself. Andy Porter no longer seemed interested in harassing Ben, but had Willie in his sights. And Andy was sneaky. I was sure Miss Hendricks would punish him if she could catch him at it or even get a witness to his crimes, but after Ben's broken nose, no one would step forward. And what were Andy's crimes?

Stealing and breaking pencils, tripping other kids on the playground, name-calling, threats, and the list went on. Even lunches went missing. I watched him go out of his way to run into Willie and then curse him for being clumsy. Willie seemed to shrug it off each time. I could see he was troubled, but he wasn't afraid either.

With these events I decided that I was ready to end my self-imposed isolation from Willie and find out what was going on in his mind. The last Sunday in September presented the opportunity to do just that. It was the monthly church pot-luck. On this 'special' Sunday, our class could smell the hot-dishes as they warmed in the oven.

There were two serving tables crowded with fried chicken, roasts, mashed potatoes, potato salad, green beans, corn, squash, pickles, ham sandwiches, and an assortment of fruit pies. Rup McClaren brought sweet cider and there were also big pots of coffee.

Pastor Potter got our attention and we all bowed as he prayed for the meal. "Dear Heavenly Father, we thank Thee for this day, we thank Thee for this food. Wilt Thou bless it to our use. Forgive us our wrongs. This we pray in Jesus' name, amen."

We all repeated the 'amen' and the line began to move slowly. We all brought our own plates and silver-ware from home. Willie was behind me and I was busy trying to plot out how I was going to get him alone so I could talk to him.

"Doesn't that chicken look crispy?" Lila nearly drooled. "I hope there's cherry pie!"

The noise never rose to an uncomfortable level, and I could pick out bits of conversations here and there. One in particular caught my attention.

"Yes. We took some bread over there the other day and invited them to church today. They don't belong anywhere! Can you imagine that! It's no wonder they're having trouble with that boy."

I wondered who 'that boy' was as I scanned the many tables for a prime spot to eat the smorgasbord on my plate. Finding none, I opted for our little class area under the stairs. Lila followed and behind her was Willie.

We sat in the same spaces we always occupied.

"Where did you get that finger roll?" she asked, looking at Willie's plate.

"You want it?"

She stood up, "I'll get my own. I forgot something to drink."

He pointed with his fork, "You see where Muriel Iverson is? Well the rolls are right in front of her and the cider is in those pitchers by the kitchen door."

She headed off in the direction of the finger rolls. Willie and I sat in silence as we surveyed the food on our plates.

"Hildi?"

I looked at him. When was the last time I'd heard him say my name?

"When you get done eating, do you wanna walk home with me?"

"Sure." I said it casually, but inside I was all butterflies and summersaults.

I really tried to eat slowly but it was hard. Lila came back with a glass of cider and a finger roll and news that there were not one, but three cherry pies. As soon as Willie cleaned his plate, he got up and headed back for a slice.

I waited a moment and then turned to Lila, "Willie asked to walk me home today."

"Good. Don't eat too much!" she grinned.

Six months ago she would have had a different reaction. But we had both changed. Now, instead of jealousy, she supported me, and I her.

***

"You ready?" He asked.

Our church had a unique, semi-round porch on the south entrance to our little church where the men usually gathered after services. Willie sat by himself leaning against one of the posts that supported the roof and looked up at me.

"I guess so." I stepped down onto the grass and we walked to the gravel road that led into the valley.

It was a good five-mile walk, but it was a warm day with the sunniest of skies. This wasn't the first time we had walked home together after church. There had been many times before, but it was the first time in a long time and the first time since I began struggling with feelings that were growing and changing.

"We haven't really talked since I came back." He began as we crunched down the road.

"I know. I think that's my fault."

He shook his head, "No ... I don't know ... maybe a little. But it's mine, too."

He picked up a rock and threw it, "My stupid sister! She told you about Ramona!"

There it was. I took a deep breath as the moment of truth arrived. I tried to sound like it didn't matter.

"Who is she?"

"Her pa owns the Rawlins Ranch, Ramona Rawlins."

He stopped and threw another rock.

"I hear she sends you letters every Saturday. I hope they're nice letters or are they full of mysterious messages?" I attempted to lighten things up, referring to the mysterious notes Willie received last summer. Those notes had been threatening.

He smiled at the memory, "No. They're 'nice' compared to *those* letters."

We walked some more and I waited until he went on.

"She's fifteen."

"Oh," I said, "an older woman."

"Yeah. And *very* pretty." He stressed 'very'. I felt a pang of jealousy but fought it off.

"You like her."

"What's not to like," he said it sarcastically.

I was surprised by his tone.

"Why do you say it like that?"

He turned suddenly. "Why didn't you write?"

I froze, dazed. "I ... I don't know." I stumbled over my words as I searched for an explanation.

"Maybe it was the headaches. I wasn't supposed to do anything the first couple of weeks, just lay around. I couldn't even read or listen to the radio.   ... maybe I was miffed that you weren't here ... but *you* didn't write *either*."

He nodded, "I know. And that's what started it. She was hanging around me a lot. She asked me if I had a girlfriend. I told her that my best friend is a girl. Then she started in. Wondered why you weren't writing. I told her I didn't know. So she told me that if *she* was my best friend, and a girl, she would be writing every day and that the post office would run out of stamps she'd write so much! It wore on me, Hildi!

"So, we started horseback riding together. Ethan told me I oughta go with her. He said I was makin' a good impression on the boss. Well, this one day we'd been out riding and took a mountain trail up into the Bitterroots. She took off ahead of me and I lost sight of her. All of a sudden her horse comes tearing back past me without her. I galloped on and found her on the ground, knocked out cold. Her horse ran back to the barn and I managed to get her home. I practically carried her and finally got her to wake up. She told me a cougar spooked her horse and threw her. So, I put her on my horse and we rode the rest of the way. After that, she wouldn't leave me alone. She told me I was her hero."

That hit home for I'd felt the same way. But there was something he hadn't told me and I was curious.

"Did you kiss her?"

"Hildi!"

"Well? Did you?"

He looked hard at me, "*She* kissed *me*! All right? And now I can't get rid of her!"

I cocked my head, "How's that?"

"I couldn't tell her to vamoose when I was on the ranch because Ethan works for her pa. I didn't want him to lose his job!"

"I don't think he would lose his job ... "

"You don't know this girl, Hildi. Yes, she's pretty, and she can ride as good as any man, but she's ..." he hunted for the word, "she's a manipulator! She's used to getting her own way. And mean! When she don't get her way, she gets downright scary. Oh, I'll admit, the first week after her accident was kind of exciting, but then she thought I belonged to her ... gee whiz! I couldn't wait to get out of there!"

We walked on and were silent. I hadn't asked to hear about Ramona, but he told me. I let everything settle in. And yet I still had questions of my own, questions that didn't have anything to do with Ramona Rawlins.

"Willie, Andy Porter is a bully. I heard what you said when he challenged you."

He nodded, "I've been talkin' to my pa about him. I'm not gonna start any fight with Andy Porter. If I get backed into a corner I might have to. But my pa says that I need to avoid it as much as I can."

I grimaced, "It's not getting any better! If something doesn't change pretty soon, I'll pound him myself! And have you seen Miss Hendricks? I think he's getting to her, too."

"I know. But Hildi, his brothers are the same way and just as crafty at shifting the blame to somebody else. The teachers in the high school wouldn't hesitate to do something, but they can't catch them. And their pa is going through a lot with that job. Kathy brings home all the gossip in town."

I regarded him skeptically, "You wouldn't have been this way last year. You woulda stood up to him even if it meant a fight!"

"Last year I hadn't known a man who chose hell over heaven ... and then went there! Hildi, Emmit Romney wasn't always a villain. Maybe someone needed to show him patience and kindness and the love of Jesus. Maybe if someone had, he wouldn't have been the murderer he was."

But I wasn't convinced, "Who says someone didn't?"

He shrugged his shoulders and shoved his hands in his pockets. "I gotta try. I gotta try with Andy Porter.   Everything we're studying in

Sunday school: Love is patient, love is kind ... I'm just tryin' to put it into practice."

We continued along as the road turned down into the valley. The once green canopy was all golden and red and orange. We weren't too far from the old town road that led to the sugar camp. In the distance was the bluff Lila and I climbed last spring. I still had a couple more questions and slowly worked up the courage to ask them.

"First kiss?"

"Huh?"

"Was that your first kiss, *William*?" I teased.

"Yup."

"And?"

"And what?"

"What was it like?"

He stopped and studied me a moment. Then said, "Let's just say it wasn't exactly how I imagined my first kiss."

His expression unsettled me, but I still had one more question.

"Did you miss me?"

There was that look again where just the slightest hint of a smile could be detected, "What do you think?"

Chapter Eleven

"Here's an article in the Clarion about the Crenshaw house." Granddad laid the paper on our kitchen table. "Hershel Dobkins is putting a 'hold' on the renovation."

Granddad was on his way out to the barn to help Daddy with the morning milking. Daddy was already in the barn and the rest of us were waiting for our breakfast. I picked up the paper and read the headline.

Curse of the Crenshaw House?

I began reading while other voices at the table dared to distract me.

Local real estate investor, Hershel Dobkins, has ceased the renovation on the Crenshaw house until further notice. Dobkins refused to comment on the circumstances of the halt, but local citizens have been well aware of the many workplace accidents that have befallen the construction crew. Rueben Porter and his sons are the lone workers after several employees walked off the job last week. One of these men, who asked not to be identified, stated that he was not going to 'be next'. Porter has been determined to see the renovation through, but after Dobkins' statement, he has put a lock on the front door of the once-stately mansion and is beginning work on another project on the eastern side of the state.

"Does this mean the Porters will move back to Ridgeview?" I asked and handed the paper to Lila who began scanning the front page.

"Might," Granddad remarked, "I guess that depends."

Mom finished the last pancake and set the platter on the table along with smoked sausages, butter, and maple syrup from our own trees.

"On what?" asked Ben.

"On what happens in October. You see, it will be fifty years ago this October that Crenshaw hung himself and some say that his ghost will visit the house on that anniversary."

"I don't like this conversation," stated mother sternly. "You don't need to fill your heads with nonsense about ghosts and curses! You children bow your heads and we'll pray over this food."

But after what I had read, both in the old papers discovered in the attic and in this current one, that was exactly what filled my head. More than ever, I wanted to ask Andy Porter what *he* knew.

***

The woodpile near the school had grown since Andy and Norm received their punishment. We were a little surprised that their dads supported the teacher. I guess we expected Andy to be so spoiled that he would find a way to get out of having to stay late after school and split wood. That being said, he didn't seem to show any more respect for Miss Hendricks and continued to bully other students. But we girls were not sitting idly by. We would take matters into our own hands. We were just waiting for the right opportunity.

"Good morning," said an unfamiliar voice from the doorway of our one-room schoolhouse. We looked up to see a smiling young gentleman in a dark blue, pin-striped suit.

"Hi," answered my brothers in unison. "Who are you?"

The man smiled and walked down the steps towards us. There was nothing about him that stood out except that he seemed overdressed and probably took too much time combing his thick brown hair.

"I'm Mr. Arnold, your substitute teacher. Miss Hendricks' father is very ill and she is spending the week in Prairie du Chien."

We had never had a man teacher before. Instead of staying inside and working at his desk like Miss Hendricks did every morning, he sat on the steps and greeted the students as they arrived. He smiled all the time and shook everyone's hands. But when it was time to ring the bell, he didn't do it.

He gathered everyone together and said, "OK, is this everybody? Let's start the day right." Then he took off his jacket and laid it over the railing.

"We'll start by forming lines by grades facing me."

He lined us up in straight lines with the first grade in front and the eighth grade in back. "We'll start with some calisthenics."

"Calliss-what?" Shorty Shimshack struggled with the word.

"Calisthenics," Mr. Arnold repeated, "Exercises!"

He stretched his arms straight out and took a wide stance. Then he bent over and touched the opposing toes, right hand, left toes; left hand right toes, all the time keeping his arms and legs stiff and only bending at the waist. We just watched him because we'd never done anything like this before. He noticed right away.

"Well don't just stand there! Hop to it! One and two and three and four and ..." away he counted and we tried to copy him, but we were pretty clumsy.

After about five minutes of that he stood up and surveyed us. His mouth still smiled, but his eyes were hard and maybe even a bit sarcastic, "Nice! Very nice! Don't you feel better? It's important to get the blood pumping in the morning. Now, some jumping jacks!"

And he jumped up in the air, bringing his hands together over his head.

I wondered if he thought we hadn't worked hard enough that morning with some of us walking as far as two miles to school both downhill and up. And a lot of us had to get up before daylight to do our chores and then wash the cow-barn smell off and eat breakfast before arriving at school.

We spent twenty minutes hopping around, running in place, and clapping our hands before we went inside. I noticed that Andy had caught on to everything this man had us do as if he'd done it before. We went inside to our desks, stood beside them, as was our custom, and waited for Mr. Arnold to start the Pledge of Allegiance.

"You may be seated." He stated and we looked at each other.

"Mister," little Gracie McClaren, who was small for her age and had to wear thick glasses, spoke up. "Mister, did you forget?"

The man looked startled, "Your name is?"

"My name is Gracie Mae McClaren and I am seven years old." She stated.

He walked up to her, knelt down on one knee, and smiled, "What did I forget, Gracie Mae McClaren?"

"You forgot the Pledge of Allegiance and the Lord's Prayer. We say it first thing every day."

Now, not all schools were exactly like ours. Some schools prayed only over their meals and some didn't pray at all. But ours had always started the day with prayer.

His expression changed to what I can only explain as a 'false pout', and he reached out and tapped the tip of her nose, "Well, Gracie Mae McClaren, you do not need to do that while I'm here!"

We looked at each other in surprise. He stood up and gazed upon us with that grin, "While I am your teacher, you will be free to express yourselves as you please! Now, instead of the Pledge of Allegiance and prayer, I have chosen a poem to start our day."

"Excuse me, sir." I recognized Willie's voice behind me.

Mr. Arnold shifted his gaze to where my friend stood, "And what is your name, young man."

"William Cooper, sir ... Willie Cooper. I don't mean no disrespect, sir, but we want to say the 'Pledge' and we like to pray."

And there were nods of agreement, maybe because this man had us doing things we weren't accustomed to, but nonetheless, most of us didn't like the changes he'd made so far.

"*'Any'* respect is the proper form of grammar. And I appreciate your boldness, William. But not everyone here agrees with you."

"Excuse me, sir, but you'd be speaking about yourself, not us."

We all looked at each other. I knew these kids, knew their families, and with the exception of Andy Porter, I knew they were all church-going people.

The grin faded and color began to spread up Mr. Arnold's neck in red blotches.

"Thank you, Mr. Cooper. Take your seat." The grin was gone as Mr. Arnold dismissed Willie.

The poem Mr. Arnold read had something to do with trees and mountains and the wisdom of the ages but nothing about God or our country. I didn't pay very close attention. Instead, I prayed.

***

Willie and I had been sitting together eating our lunches outside under one of the many majestic oak trees that surrounded the schoolhouse and dotted the schoolyard. The leaves were a thick, colorful aromatic carpet on the ground. We tried to enjoy our lunch as we talked about the new substitute teacher and wondered what other changes he had in store for us.

"Cooper!" hollered, Andy, "Hey, Cooper! You a Bible-banger?"

When Andy approached, Willie did his best to ignore him.

"Hey, I'm talkin' to you!" But there was something strange about the way Andy spoke.

"I heard you." Willie answered quietly.

Andy seemed louder than normal and Norm trailed behind him.

"What's goin' on over here? You two up to somethin'?" Andy stumbled and caught himself.

Willie jumped up and grabbed the bigger boy to steady him, not to start anything. "What's the matter with you?"

Andy shook him off, "Nothin's the matter! You do that again and I'll knock your head off!"

"You've been drinkin'!" Willie exclaimed, "I can smell it on your breath!"

Andy was a lot bigger than either of us. He grabbed a fist full of Willie's shirt and threw him up against the tree. "You tell and I'll fix you!"

I jumped up, ready to fight just as Andy let him go. "Cooper, you think you're something around here. I can see it in how you walk and how you talk. You're such a coward! But don't worry, your girl here's gonna fight for you!"

They walked away, back towards the building, kicking up leaves as they went. I looked at Willie and he looked at me.

"Too many changes," he said at last.

"Yup." I agreed.

"Hard to love somebody like that."

"Love your enemies." I said.

"... and pray for those who persecute you," he added.

Neither Willie nor I told Mr. Arnold about Andy. The rest of the day held no more surprises than the morning and we were glad to get back to the books.

Chapter Twelve

"Mr. Arnold just graduated from the university. Give him a chance, Hildi. He's just new. I'm sure tomorrow he'll settle down, and by Friday you'll forget all about today." Daddy tried to assure me that our new teacher would come around, but I wasn't so sure.

"You know, these fellows who go away to universities, they come back with all sorts of new-fangled notions." Daddy had the manure fork and was digging for earthworms. Friday morning, he, Chet Cooper, Uncle Jerry, and Granddad would load up the car with fishing gear and head up north for two days of fishing. That would leave just us women and children to do the chores. Daddy almost cancelled the trip, but Mom insisted that we would be all right.

"But he has us doing exercises before school and he didn't have us say the 'pledge' or even let us pray!"

Daddy quit digging, "Hmm. Don't know if I like that. Maybe I'll have to stop in and talk to him. I think he's staying at the Boarding House in Cedar Grove."

He turned over a forkful of earth and quickly snatched a large earthworm as it tried to wriggle away. Nearby was an old tin can where Daddy placed the bait. There is something about telling your problem to someone who can do something about it that sets a mind at ease. I was glad I had my daddy.

***

The next morning we were again met by Mr. Arnold. He wore the same suite that he'd had on the previous day. He also wore the same smile. I was still uneasy but anxious to see if anything had changed after Daddy's visit with him the night before. Again, Mr. Arnold did not ring the school bell, and again, we had to do exercises; but this time, they were easier.

We followed him in to the school where he gestured for us to take our seats.

"Boys and girls, I had a visitor last night."

I tried not to smile, thinking of my father.

"This well-meaning man insisted that saying the Pledge of Allegiance and the Lord's Prayer is an important part of your day. I am here to tell you that although I appreciate his coming to see me, I still do not see it that way. Yet, if there is a volunteer who still wishes to carry on this '*tradition*,'" he raised his fingers to make quotation marks in the air, "he or she may lead it."

Mr. Arnold fixed his eyes on me, and I knew it was a challenge since it had been my father who talked to him. I knew I had to stand in order to take a stand. Just as I was about to, I heard someone standing up behind me.

"I will," Johnny Iverson said.

"Very well," remarked Mr. Arnold. "If you want to do this, you may. But you don't *have* to."

We all stood, all except Andy, and recited the pledge and the prayer. When we were done, we sat quietly and waited for Mr. Arnold to proceed.

"With that out of the way, take out the arithmetic problems I assigned yesterday and we will proceed."

Mr. Arnold seemed a strange sort of teacher. Oh, he knew his subjects very well, maybe even better than Miss Hendricks. But I could not understand why he held prayer and the

Pledge of Allegiance in contempt. I didn't know if I liked this new type of teacher. Miss Hendricks had been to what they called a 'normal school'. She only had to go two years to be our teacher. Mr. Arnold told us he had gone to the university for four years and had a Bachelors degree.

The next couple of days seemed to go pretty smooth. However, it was clear that Mr. Arnold didn't like Willie. He wouldn't call on him and seemed to look past him when he raised his hand. Conversely, he gave Andy lots of attention. One day at lunch, I overheard Andy telling Mr. Arnold about the Crenshaw house and its history. Andy was really pretty smart. He talked about the design of the house, how the limestone had been quarried and what work had been finished. Most of the floors had been torn out and walls removed that had been erected to make apartments. He told them of his brothers going to work for his dad when the rest of the crew walked off the job. Mr. Arnold was intrigued.

"What a fascinating story! So, your brothers and your father are restoring this haunted house?"

"Were," answered Andy, "Mr. Dobkins had them stop. He's worried about what might happen in October. Fifty years ago, close to

Halloween was when August Crenshaw hung himself from the balcony. I guess ol' Hershel thinks the house has ghosts."

"With everything you've told me, I think I would agree!"

Mr. Arnold had taken a shine to Andy and Norm. Oh, it helped that Norm brought him a small apple pie. He'd done this once for Miss Hendricks, but she had looked him right in the eye and said, "This is not going to raise your grade, Mr. Tucker."

But Mr. Arnold was ecstatic and cut right into it at lunchtime the very next day which happened to be Thursday. And while he enjoyed his pie, we watched Andy and Norm disappear behind the outhouse.

"What do you think?" Stella Johnson inquired. "They're either going to smoke or take a drink."

Willie, Johnny Iverson, and a couple other boys were playing marbles with Johnny doing most of the winning. Johnny might not have been very good at baseball or arithmetic, but he was the best at marbles and everyone knew it.

Mr. Arnold had a small thermos and poured himself a cup of coffee to have with his pie. He had on a different suit today. It was brown and double-breasted and he wore a red-flowered silk tie. As soon as he finished his coffee, he rose from his seat on the steps and went inside. It was then that Norm and Andy returned from behind the outhouse. I watched as they meandered towards the marble players. Johnny lay on his belly as he took aim with his shooter.

"Iverson! You stealing marbles again?" Taunted Andy.

Johnny didn't look up or say anything but carefully aimed, and just as he was about to shoot, Norm tapped his elbow with his toe. That sent Johnny's marble careening out of the circle and onto the grass.

"That's all right, Johnny. You can go again," said Willie, but I could hear the irritation in his voice.

"That's all right, Johnny," repeated Andy, "you can go again! You gonna let 'im cheat, Cooper? He cheated me out of all my marbles last week!"

"Yeah! And he's got most of mine, too!" added Norm.

Johnny sat up. "I won your marbles fair and square! I don't cheat, Norm, and you know it!"

For a moment, Norm looked ashamed.

"You callin' me a liar, four-eyes? Why don't you stand up here and maybe I'll fix your glasses for you!"

Johnny took the challenge. He was just as tall as Andy but all gangly and awkward. In one quick move, Andy grabbed Johnny's glasses and gave him a push, sending him to the ground on top of the marbles.

"Give me back my glasses!" cried Johnny.

"What, these glasses? I just won 'em like you won my marbles! They're mine now. Only thing is, I can't see out of 'em."

Andy threw his hands out in front of him like a blind man. He pretended to grasp the air in front of him while Norm laughed nervously.

It was then that I knew we had to stop it. Lila, Barb, and I had talked about it, but now Stella was ready to attack this bully, too. We stood up as a group and began to march across the schoolyard when I saw Willie step in front of Andy.

"That's enough! Give Johnny his glasses."

Andy froze, dropped his hands and peered through the thick lenses at Willie.

"Whatcha gonna do, Cooper?"

"Give – them—back." He stressed each word and we stopped in our tracks.

Andy regarded the entire group with spite. He took the glasses off slowly, never taking his eyes off Willie, and tossed them in the dirt.

"My glasses!" screeched Johnny, and as he stooped to pick them up, Andy kicked him hard in the backside, sending him into the dirt face-first.

That was all it took. Before another word could be said, Willie flew at Andy and the two were a tumbling ball of fists and grunts. But it was easy to see that even though Andy was bigger, he was outmatched. Willie was wiry-all muscle and speed-and his fists were connecting.

"Stop it!" A voice shouted, "Stop this fighting at once!"

Mr. Arnold came running full throttle and reached in with both hands to tear the two apart. They continued to punch and tear at each other until he had them both standing on their feet, and even then, Willie got in another swing. Mr. Arnold gave them both a good shaking.

"Oh there will be consequences for this!" he shouted and there was no missing the rage in his voice.

Andy's nose and lips were bleeding and one eye was red. Willie, except for a torn shirt and being covered in dirt, appeared to be unscathed. Mr. Arnold poured over Andy's injuries, even pulled out a crisp white handkerchief and handed it to him.

Then he turned on Willie, "You! You ruffian in sheep's clothing! Look what you've done to this boy!"

Willie's eyes grew wide, "Mr. Arnold, he's been asking for it! He took Johnny's ... "

"You will be silent!" screamed Mr. Arnold. He grabbed Willie by the collar and marched him to the schoolhouse. We stood in stunned silence except for the snuffling of Andy as he coped with his bloody nose.

When Mr. Arnold reached the schoolhouse steps, he turned and yelled at us, "Come on! You will all witness this!"

He moved with such force and purpose that he practically dragged Willie up the steps. We followed in haste and I wondered what was about to happen. Andy stopped at the pump to wash the blood off his face.   When we entered the classroom, Mr. Arnold still had Willie by the shirt collar. He was parked in the front of the room next to the teacher's large wooden desk.

"Take your seats. Now!" Mr. Arnold released Willie, ordered him to stay put, and turned to the cupboard behind the desk. For an instant, Willie's eyes met mine, but he looked away quickly. The teacher rummaged around briefly and found what he was looking for. But it wasn't the paddle. When he turned back to us, he held a long, wooden stick that appeared to have been recently cut from a willow tree. It was a thick switch and all the bark had been peeled off, making it slick and pliable.

He walked around Willie to face us.

"You will know this: As long as I am here, fighting will *not* be tolerated." His eyes were savage as he directed the next sentence towards Willie, "And he who throws the first punch will be dealt with most severely!"

He held the stick in both hands and flexed it. "You've all heard the old adage, *Spare the rod, spoil the child.* Well, my father made sure my brothers and I heard it ... over and over again! He taught me very well. I cut this yesterday. I had a feeling I would be needing it."

Lila was on her feet in an instant, "But Willie didn't start it! It was Andy! Andy's the bully!"

She was joined by others, but Mr. Arnold refused to listen. "No! You will sit down, young lady! All of you! Be quiet! Mr. Porter's injuries are substantial and as I look at a boy of Mr. Porter's size, do you really expect me to believe that he could take such a beating if Mr. Cooper had not attacked him first? Had not ambushed him? No! I do not believe you!"

Willie just stood there, not really looking at anybody, not even me, and worse yet, not even speaking up to defend himself. The front of his red plaid shirt was un-tucked, and there was a long rip along the buttons. Dirt smudged his face, yet, he somehow came across as strong and brave.

"Bend over and put your hands on my desk, Mr. Cooper." Mr. Arnold seemed to regain his composure.

Willie didn't move for a moment but took a deep breath. Getting spanked in front of the class was humiliating and Miss Hendricks always saved it for the most grievous offenses. And Willie was not perfect. Over the years he'd been in fights, had even caused them. Miss Hendricks had punished him for them and that usually consisted of making him stay late to chop kindling. But this time, he had not been in the wrong. He was defending Johnny and this punishment didn't seem fair. We weren't aware of how Mr. Arnold was going to use the 'rod', but I assumed that a spanking with a thick switch was meant to sting the backside more than a paddle. But, I was about to learn that my assumptions were wrong.

"Come on, Cooper! Take your punishment!" Norm repeated Willie's admonition to Andy from the day Miss Hendricks used the paddle on Andy's backside.

Willie obeyed without being ordered a second time. Mr. Arnold took off his suit-coat, rolled up his sleeves, and loosened his tie. Then, with his full strength he laid the rod across

Willie's *back*, not his backside! It made a sharp smack. Willie recoiled with that blow and a look of disbelief appeared on his face. The room seemed to gasp with the first lash. Mr. Arnold waited for Willie to recover his stance and once more brought the stick down with the same force. Again Willie bravely took it. Maybe we were as shocked as he was, for we sat there in stunned silence, unable to do anything but stare at what was taking place. Over and over, Mr. Arnold struck him until the total number came to thirteen, one blow for each year of age. We watched Willie as he tried to keep from crying out, but, in the end he couldn't help it. His legs shook violently and his breathing was ragged. Mr. Arnold was sweating. We were crying softly and many had looked away. In the doorway of the building stood a figure; it was Andy. He had not been there for the entire ordeal but had only come in for the last three blows and had seen its effects. His eye had quickly swollen as did his lip and nose.   But despite the disfigurement, everyone saw their own horror expressed in Andy's face.

Mr. Arnold noticed him where he stood and said in triumph, "There, Mr. Porter, is justice for your injuries."

He turned back to Willie, "Take your seat, Mr. Cooper."

Willie continued to lean on the desk and I could see his arms trembling. His face was flushed and his eyes were watering. He turned his head and wiped them on his sleeves, then, slowly attempted to straighten up.

"Today, Mr. Cooper! Move! You're not that bad off."

Willie turned towards the class, took a step, and lost his balance; but as he tripped, Andy Porter was there and caught him. Willie bit his lip and winced when Andy put his arm around his shoulders. Mr. Arnold's eyes widened as he watched.

"Porter! He's shamming, let him alone. He's fine! " Mr. Arnold demanded.

But Andy didn't pay any attention to him as he helped Willie to his desk. I turned just in time to hear Andy say under his breath, "This don't make us even, Cooper."

Chapter Thirteen

We waited after school for Willie. He wasn't allowed to go outside for recess, and he had to stay an extra hour after school as if the beating he'd taken hadn't been enough punishment. Mr. Arnold sent Andy Porter home early in case his nose was broken. Finally, the door opened and Willie emerged, moving a little slower than normal.

"Why are you all still here?"

Lila stepped beside him, "We're walking you home."

"No, you don't need to ..."

"Don't argue!" Joe cut him off.

Ben joined in, "Willie, we love you. You're like the big brother we never had!"

"Hear that, 'big brother'?" I added, "You don't have a choice."

He shook his head and smiled, "Big brother, huh? I've never been a big brother before."

We walked along and talked, mostly about Mr. Arnold and Andy Porter and everything that happened that day. Willie didn't say much and moved slower than normal. When we were about half way home, Lila stopped.

"How bad does it hurt?" She asked.

"Hardly at all." He lied. But we all could see it in his eyes.

"Willie, will you let me look?"

He slowly pulled out his shirt tail and lifted it up while the audience of four gaped. Lila took the material from him and raised it as high as his shoulders to reveal long raised welts that snaked across the skin and crisscrossed each other. Some were raw and a few oozed blood, which had been camouflaged by the colored fabric of his shirt.

"Oh, Willie ... that looks so painful!" She cried.

I was mute and shook my head, remembering the beating we'd witnessed. And then a thought struck me, "He planned this."

"What are you saying?"

An ember was growing in me, "I'm saying Mr. Arnold's had it in for Willie all along. Willie stood up to him on the first day and he didn't like it. He cut that 'rod' to use on him, not on anybody else, and definitely not on Andy! He just didn't have to wait for an excuse to use it!"

"Mr. Arnold is a terrible teacher!" exclaimed Ben. Now he was riled, too.

"No. Mr. Arnold is a very good teacher." Said Willie, trying to calm us down, "But he's mixed up about a lot of things. You heard what he said ... he learned from his father. He doesn't know anything about mercy-- just cruelty."

"You're defending him?" Lila asked as she carefully lowered Willie's shirt tail.

"No ... but I'm not the first kid to have a hickory stick laid across his back. A foot or two lower and I wouldn't be able to sit down and you'd be laughing instead of makin' all this fuss. Besides, I *did* throw the first punch. My pa warned me that you have to face consequences for your actions, and if I picked a fight with Andy, I'd have to face the consequences."

I remembered our conversation from Sunday. That's what he'd said then. At the time I figured the 'consequence' would be Andy getting the best of Willie, not the other way around. But I was still mad at Mr. Arnold and what he had done. Suddenly, there was a sound up ahead. There was a bend in the road and the commotion came from there. As we continued along, we saw two tall figures approaching, moving somewhat unsteadily and singing as they came.

We were soon passing each other.

"Hi," I said politely as they passed.

They were two boys who looked quite a bit older than us, and completely drunk.

"Seen any scrappy roosters?" One said.

"What do you need them for?" asked Ben innocently.

"C'mon, Ben. He doesn't mean chickens." Willie took him by the shoulder and guided him away.

But the other boy stepped in front of them, "Hold on ... hold on now. My brother and me don't mean any harm. You see, we're new around here and haven't met too many people."

He reached in his hip pocket and pulled out a half-empty pint bottle of whiskey. He bent over and looked my brother in the face.

"How 'bout a drink, kid? It'll put hair on your chest!"

Ben's eyes grew wide, "No, no thanks. We've gotta get home."

"Home!" The first one slurred, "Home sweet home!"

Willie made a move around the second boy as we waited nervously.

"Well, see ya around," the first said and slapped Willie on the back. It was a friendly slap, not hard, but it drove Willie right to the ground.

"Whoa!" the second boy said, "You cut his legs out from under him!"

I got there first and pulled him up with the intention of putting as much distance between the two intoxicated teens and ourselves as I could.

"What's the matter with 'im?" The second boy asked.

Joe spoke up, "He fought the school bully and whipped him. Then the teacher turned around and blamed him for starting the fight and beat him with a stick. But it wasn't him that started it. It was that Andy Porter!"

"Joe!" I yelled, and got Willie started down the road with Lila and Ben.

I had begun to see a similarity between the two boys and the 'school bully'. Both were tall with blond hair and blue eyes. It didn't take long for me to figure out that these were Porters, too!

"Hang on now, I'm sorry there, kid. I didn't mean to hurt you." The first one trotted after Willie followed by the other and myself. I had a bad feeling.

"You really beat up the school bully?"

"We have to go," I insisted.

"Did you say the bully's name is Porter?"

Willie pulled up short, turned, and addressed him, "You know his name."

I gestured for Lila to take the boys and keep going. "Take the old town road." I advised. It was shorter. "We'll be right behind you."

Both boys had to be as tall as Daddy which was at least six feet.

"I'm Sam Porter and this is my brother Gabe," said the first one. "You bested our little brother?"

"He had it coming," Willie declared.

"You're kind of scrawny to take Andy," One stood on each side of Willie and looked down at him.

"We never got to finish the fight ... but I was ahead."

Gabe laughed at that statement, "You were ahead! How 'bout that, Sam?"

"Let's go home, Willie," I interrupted, reached in and took him by the hand. I didn't know if they would try to stop us or not, but under my breath, I urged him to keep walking and didn't let go of him.

We walked rapidly and didn't dare turn around or speak until we rounded the bend and were out of sight. Up ahead lay the overgrown and defunct old township road. Lila and the boys were waiting for us.

"You were ahead? You were ahead! What were you thinking?" I roared dropping his hand.

"I *was* ahead!" He proclaimed, "I didn't lie, I told the truth."

***

You can bet we didn't keep what happened at school that day a secret. We verbally jostled to see who would get to tell our parents what happened. Daddy listened intently but didn't say too much about it. Of course, we were vehement and just came short of calling Mr. Arnold the anti-Christ!

We were doing our chores in the barn when we wondered out loud if Chet would go find Mr. Arnold and beat him up or if Mr. Arnold would be fired or go to jail.

"That's the kind of trouble Chet doesn't need to be starting," Daddy remarked.

"School days, school days, dear old Golden Rule days ..." Granddad sang from between the cows.

"What's that, Granddad?" Joe picked up one of the barn cats and petted it.

He stood up and came out onto the aisle that ran down the middle of the barn. "Oh, I was just remembering Mr. Solverson. He was my school teacher way back in ... well, way back when. I wasn't raised around here. I went to a different school but my, oh my, how that man would lay into us. There was a willow tree growin' down by the creek that ran near the schoolhouse, and he would go out there and cut a switch if it looked like a trouble-maker needed to be 'taught' a lesson."

I looked up at him, "You ever get 'taught' that kind of a lesson?"

"Nope. I saw what happened to the trouble-makers and was smart enough not to do anything that would get me into that kind of trouble."

Lila climbed over the gate and out of the calf pen where she had been feeding a new calf. "Mr. Arnold lost his temper. I've never seen Miss Hendricks get that angry."

"She has patience," said Ben. "It's because she's a lot older than Mr. Arnold. Like, Hildi doesn't have as much patience as Ma does."

I rolled my eyes.

Daddy listened to all of this and finally made his contribution, "How old do you think Miss Hendricks is?"

"At least forty," remarked Joe.

"Probably more," added Ben. "She's an 'old maid'."

Lila took the cat away from Joe. "No, she's not that old, maybe thirty?"

"She is twenty-eight," said Daddy. "She was engaged to a soldier before the war and he was killed. I wouldn't go around calling her an 'old maid', Ben."

All I knew was that I wanted her back.

"Are you still gonna go fishin'?" Joe asked.

Daddy took the milker off a cow and stepped into the aisle. He 'burped' the machine and took the lid off, revealing a frothy pail of milk. Granddad brought in the 'shotgun' pail (a tall pail with a lid that held around five gallons) and set it near the milking machine. Daddy then transferred the milk from his milker pail to the shotgun pail.

"I think so. Besides, sometimes men need to get away and be men. At least, these men do. We've been planning this for a long time. Jerry called this afternoon to tell us what time we needed to be there. We'll do chores tomorrow morning and you kids, your ma, and grandma will have to do them over the weekend. Think you can handle that?"

We all assured him we could.

As soon as the last milker was pulled off the last cow, we opened the barn door, released the stanchions, and turned the cows out into their night pasture. I stood in the doorway and watched them saunter away in the twilight.

Beyond the pasture and over the bluff lay the Cooper farm. I wondered what was happening there, if Willie's folks were angry with him for fighting; if they were angry with the teacher; if they were angry with Andy Porter. I would have to wait until the next day to find out. Unknown to me, my father would be making some telephone calls that night that would change Mr. Arnold's world.

Chapter Fourteen

To anyone who didn't know the intricacies of living in the bluffs, they might not understand that every valley has more little coulees that snake in between the hills and allow the spring-fed creeks a way out on their journey to the bigger rivers. The bluffs and valleys were nearly a labyrinth ... nearly, but not quite. Willie was our closest neighbor even though to take the main road to his driveway from our farm was a good three-quarter mile, and then from his driveway back to his farm was another three-quarter mile. But over the bluff and through the pastures was a third the distance. That was how I preferred to go. But on school days it wasn't an option.

Our farm was on the very edge of the township line which meant we were the farthest away from the school and had to walk exactly two miles to and from school every day. We didn't mind the walk unless it started to rain or if the snow was deep. And sometimes, if we left home later than normal, we were likely to meet classmates on the road and we'd all walk together. Since Mr. Arnold started teaching, we were leaving later and later each morning. It was turning into a bad habit that might prove hard to break.

I dreaded seeing Mr. Arnold after what had happened the previous day. In the distance I could see Willie just approaching the end of his driveway. The boys had charged on ahead.

"Hi," I greeted.

He nodded at Lila and me and joined us on the road.

"Did your daddy go after Mr. Arnold?"

Willie shook his head, "I didn't tell him."

"After what he did to you? You didn't tell him about the fight or anything?" Lila couldn't believe it.

"I told him about the fight, told him that Mr. Arnold kept me late after school, even said he thrashed me, but I didn't tell any more than that."

"But why, Willie?" she pleaded.

"I know my pa's temper. If he knew what Mr. Arnold did, he'd go after him. He might do something that could get him in trouble with the law. No, my pa don't need to know about this. He's got that fishing trip and I think he needs it like I needed to get away last summer."

Yes, I could see it. Something had changed him and for the better, and maybe it was that trip to Montana. Maybe it was working on a ranch, getting far away from violent memories. Maybe it was meeting a girl named Ramona who gave him his first kiss, and maybe it was good for us to be apart for a while.

"But is it better today?" Lila asked, "The pain, I mean."

He nodded, "Yeah, a lot better. I can't hide anything from Betty. She ended up seeing my back and made me tell her what happened. She got some stuff and put it on those welts and I made her promise not to tell Pa."

***

Mr. Arnold was not waiting for us outside when we all arrived. The door was open and his car was parked outside. We milled around not daring to go in, not wanting to face him. Willie and I sat down on the steps and watched as a car drove up and let Andy Porter out.

He ambled right up to Willie and stood there a moment. Both locked eyes, stone-faced.

"How's your back, Cooper?"

"It's all right. I'm sorry about your face, Andy." Willie sounded sincere.

"Nose isn't broken. Everything's just fine."

"You still not gonna let this go?"

"Can't. Porters get even."

"Good morning!" Mr. Arnold emerged from the school house, carrying the peeled stick he had used the previous day. "It is time to begin. Form your lines for calisthenics."

His smile was as bright as it had been the first day we met him. He was back in the blue pinstripe suit. He took the jacket off and once again laid it over the railing along the schoolhouse steps.

"This last day we will be more rigorous. You all seem to have caught on to the exercises, and I'm sure you will want to continue them after I leave."

Either he didn't see our looks of horror, or he ignored them. Before beginning, he pulled Andy aside and confidentially told him that he could sit out, "Don't need to get that nose bleeding again with all this jumping around."

We began with the toe-touches, then the jumping jacks, followed by running in place. When that was done, he had us get a partner and do sit-ups. For the girls in dresses, this was very uncomfortable. I was next to Willie and any time we had to stretch or bend, which was just about all the time, he caught his breath. I knew he was still smarting from the day before, no matter what he'd told us earlier.

"All right, everyone, down for pushups!"

We watched him get down and pump his arms, lifting his body like a board.

Many tried it but couldn't get the hang of it. Joe and Ben were the exception. Competitive in everything, they went up and down like a couple of see-saws.

"Wonderful! Feel that blood pumping, those lungs expanding! Come on now, everyone at least try!"

We tried but, boy, were we glad when he let us stop trying.

"That's it. Everyone inside."

Mr. Arnold picked up his stick and his jacket and jogged up the steps. For some reason we did not follow him with the same energy.

We stood by our desks ready to follow our routine, a routine which we thought Mr. Arnold finally understood. But instead of asking for a volunteer, he flexed his stick playfully and sat on the edge of the desk.

"Sit down, please. I want to talk to you about yesterday."

This might be interesting. I wondered if Mr. Arnold had regretted punishing Willie so severely. Perhaps he was about to admit his mistake and tell us that he was going to turn over a new leaf.

"Yesterday's display on the playground was out of line, even brutal."

He spoke the words slowly and carefully while turning the stick ever so slowly in his hands. "I was dismayed at the injuries inflicted, may I say even shocked."

He looked up. Was he talking about the fight or what he did to Willie? This didn't exactly sound like a repentant man.

"I hope you will understand that disobedience and displays of violence will be met with the same severity as it was yesterday. I hope you all have learned from witnessing Mr. Cooper's punishment."

He stood up and placed the stick next to the desk, "Now, the poem I've chosen to start the day …"

Gracie Mae McClaren raised her little hand as he continued to talk. She really was not much bigger than her desk even though her age said otherwise. Soon the little hand was waving back and forth and someone cleared his throat which made Mr. Arnold look up.

"What is it?"

Someone pointed at Gracie Mae.

"Yes, Gracie?"

She stood up and looked at him over the top of her glasses, "Excuse me, Mr. Arnold. You forgot again."

But this time he didn't approach her, didn't kneel down, and didn't give her that toothy grin.

"No, I didn't."

He pulled a book from his bag, turned to a marked page and began to read, but as he did, a tiny voice interrupted him.

"I pledge allegiance ..."

It was Gracie Mae McClaren. I quickly joined her and within seconds everyone was on their feet with hands over their hearts, facing the flag and reciting the Pledge ... even Andy.

Mr. Arnold snapped the book shut, tucked it under his arm, and had a most disgusted look on his face.

"All right. Let's move on." He said abruptly.

"Our Father, who art in Heaven ..."

This time it was Willie's voice, and we finished our prayer. Everyone sat down with the exception of Willie who stood facing Mr. Arnold. Neither moved and we all held our breath. I wondered if Willie realized he might be inviting another whipping. But at long last Mr. Arnold opened his mouth.

"That will do Mr. Cooper. Take your seat."

Willie obeyed and the standoff was over. Mr. Arnold collected the homework from the previous day and sat correcting it. We busied ourselves on other assignments when we heard the sound of a loud engine and the slamming of two car doors. Everyone looked up to see who was coming in.

To our amazement and delight, we recognized Miss Hendricks. We were all aglow and turned to each other to share our joy at the return of our teacher. She strode up to the desk where Mr. Arnold sat. He looked up and did not seem to know who she was.

"May I help you?" He asked benignly.

"You are sitting at my desk, Mr. Arnold."

He was taken aback, "Pardon me?"

"I am Miss Hendricks and you are sitting at my desk."

Fred Randall stood in the doorway, watching Miss Hendricks with interest. Fred was a young farmer and veteran. It was his car outside and everyone knew he'd taken quite a shine to her. The feeling was mutual. She acknowledged him and nodded. He stepped inside the classroom, crossed his arms, and waited.

"Mr. Arnold, I think it best if we step into the alcove to continue this conversation."

He got up and followed her into the small entrance where we hung our coats and stored wood for the wood stove. We could still see them, but we had to strain to hear what was being said.

"Last night I received a telephone call from one of the students in this room. First she told me about the changes you've made. Then she told me about yesterday."

We looked around at each other. Stella Johnson had a knowing look and I instantly knew that she was the one who had made that call. It was the first time I ever wanted to hug her!

Miss Hendricks stepped back inside the classroom and her eyes settled on Willie, "William Cooper, come up here."

Willie got up, crossed the room, and stepped into the alcove.

"Turn around and lift up your shirt, please."

He gingerly pulled out his shirt tail and lifted it as much as he could. Miss Hendricks took hold of the clothing, raised it up higher, and stared at the marks.

"Good heavens," she whispered, "Fred, come here."

Fred stepped behind Willie. His eyes narrowed and he shook his head. Finally, Miss Hendricks lowered the shirt tail and told Willie to go back to his seat. Then she marched to the teacher's desk where the peeled stick appeared to be on display. She lifted it, turned it round, and ran her hand down its length. She returned to the alcove and faced Mr. Arnold.

"Is this what you used on the boy?" her voice rose enough so that we could hear her clearly.

"I see *you* have a paddle in the closet." His volume matched hers.

"That was not the question, Mr. Arnold. Is this stick what you used on that boy?"

"What if it is?"

"There is a fine line between punishment and what was described to me as nothing less than brutality--torture. Thirteen times, Mr. Arnold? You beat this boy with your *full force* thirteen times? He could barely make it to his seat afterword! That is abuse, Mr. Arnold, not punishment!"

Mr. Arnold showed no remorse but held his head up high. I noticed that his ears had turned very red and red blotches covered his neck.

"Mr. Arnold, I ask you to get your things and leave."

"I've been hired for the week!" he said defiantly.

"And I'm telling you from the chairman of the school board: your teaching days at this school are over. Fred, help Mr. Arnold on his way."

Within minutes Mr. Arnold removed himself from our presence. Fred Randall walked behind him to make sure he didn't forget anything and Miss Hendricks stood in the doorway holding the stick and tapping it on the floor every so often.

"He's gone." Fred stated when he returned.

Miss Hendricks turned away in a private moment, "Thanks, Fred. I'll see you later."

He departed and she walked to her desk, still holding the stick. When she was centered in front of us, she broke it over her knee and threw it into the waste paper basket.

***

We were thrilled to have Miss Hendricks back. Even Andy seemed glad to see her. The entire atmosphere lightened with her return and we smiled all that day and laughed easily. Everyone wanted to spend time with our teacher. But the littlest ones won out. They surrounded her as she ate her lunch, and we went back to doing what we always did. I stayed near Willie. We sat on the steps with Johnny Iverson while we tried to decide what game we could get going. The day had grown cooler and we wouldn't be able to enjoy our outside lunches much longer.

"Don't any of you guys own a football?" It was Andy and Norm.

Johnny looked at Willie and Willie looked at me. I looked back at Andy, "Do you?"

He nodded, "Yeah. I'll bring it next week." He paused, "You do know how to play football ..."

No one knew all the rules. Most of us had never seen a football game. But we'd heard them on the radio.

"We'll figure it out."

Andy had been standing but now he squatted down close to Willie, "I don't get you, Cooper."

"I could say the same thing." He responded.

"You won't fight me. You walk away. I do something to four-eyes here and you turn into a torpedo. Just when I had you figured as a coward, you turn into a hero."

Johnny spoke up, "You don't know anything about Willie. Why just last March, he and Hildi ..."

Willie waved a hand, "Not now, Johnny, understand?"

"But Willie, he don't even know about ..."

"I mean it, Johnny," Willie insisted.

Andy stood back up, "Whatever, Cooper. Like I said before, we aren't 'even'."

Just then Miss Hendricks rang the bell and it was time to get back to class.

Chapter Fifteen

"Boys, remember you've got to get home and bring the cows up. Lila, I'm going to wait and walk home with Willie. I should be right behind you," I directed my siblings. Lila didn't appreciate it.

"Why can't we all walk home with Willie?"

"Just get the boys home and tell Mom I'll be there."

She turned on her heel and trudged off.

"What's the matter with her?" he asked, coming down the steps.

"Doesn't matter. Let's go."

We passed Gundersons' empty tobacco field and watched a hawk being dive-bombed by blackbirds. Ottertail Creek ran about twenty-five yards from the road and we passed a car parked nearby with out-of-state plates. Two gray-haired men in hip waders were casting lines into the shallows trying to coax big brown trout from under the rocks.

"Do you 'spose our dads are doin' that right now?" he asked.

"They're on a lake, Willie. That's a little different than fly fishing in Ottertail Creek."

"I know that," he answered, "All I meant was, do you think they're fishing now?"

"I'm sure of it. Daddy said they would be getting to the cabin about noon, so they should be fishing."

We stopped a moment when we saw that one of the men had hooked something. He pulled the line through his fingers, easing the fish towards him. We waited while he unhooked it. He pushed the straw fedora to the back of his head and looked up at us.

"You got a lot o' carp in this stream!" He held up the rough fish for us to see.

"You can eat carp, too," Willie called back.

The man looked to be about Granddad's age.

"Do you eat carp, son?"

"Yeah."

"Come down here," he beckoned.

I reminded Willie that we both had chores to do, but he told me to hush. We made our way to the little footpath the fishermen took to get to the banks of Ottertail creek. The path was exactly like a cow path, being no more than a foot wide with grass on either side. The only thing that would have made it more like a pasture would have been large, flat cow pies, but there were none.

"You two must be headed home from school." The man said as he swished through the water towards us. Under the large suspenders that held up the hip waders was a khaki military style shirt. I'd seen many of the men and boys wearing them. His gray hair peeked out from under the straw hat. His eyes were green with dark eyebrows, flecked with gray.

"Well I've got a half dozen of those carp in a gunnysack here and you're welcome to the whole thing." He reached along the bank and held up the dripping sack.

Willie looked at the bag and then at the man. "That's a lot a fish to be giving a stranger. Would you let me make a suggestion?"

"We won't be strangers if we introduce ourselves. My name is Howard Buckley. Every fall I drive up here from Lombard, Illinois, to fish for trout."

I looked downstream at the other man who looked to be of similar age as Mr. Buckley.

"I'm Will Cooper and this is my friend Hildi." Willie replied, "There's a place along the Mississippi that can smoke those carp for you. If you don't have time or can't come back for 'em, he'll trade the ones you've got for ones he's already smoked."

The man looked interested, "Smoked carp? Haven't heard of that. How does it taste?"

"It's real good." Willie replied, "You still have to pick the bones out, but you haven't wasted your time or the fish."

"Where is this place?" Mr. Buckley set his rod on the bank and deposited the fish in the sack next to it. He reached into his shirt pocket and produced a small pad and pencil. He licked the end of the pencil and prepared to write.

"It's called Amundson's Fish Market. You go back to Cedar Grove and take highway 180 west to the river. Then turn north onto state highway 35 and drive that way until you see a building on the left with a dock down into the river. There'll be a sign that says Amundson's Fish Market. He's there all day long, but I'd get there before dark if I was you."

Buckley gestured to the other man who was slowly making his way through the knee-deep water, "This lad has advised us to take these carp to a fellow who smokes them. What do you think?"

"At least it wouldn't be a wasted day." The other man took off his hat revealing a bald head and wiped his brow with his shirtsleeve. "I don't think I've ever pulled as many rough fish out of this creek as I have today!"

"This is Will and his friend Hildi. John Sherman, retired Brigadier General." Buckley said, introducing the other man.

Sherman reached out a hand to shake Willie's, "Nice to meet you, son. You too, young lady. How long of a drive would you say it is from here?"

"Maybe about half an hour," Willie replied, shading the sun from his eyes and pointing west.

John Sherman nodded. They both made their way up onto the bank with some difficulty as it was steep and muddy. Willie reached out a hand to help pull Mr. Buckley up who then turned to help his friend out in the same way.

We walked the trail, single file, back to the road where the men's late model sedan waited. They took off their waders, loaded their gear and fish into the trunk, and turned to us.

"I hear you folks up here had some excitement the last few months."

"Sir?" questioned Willie.

"Emmit Romney." John Sherman answered. "What was it, back in March he showed up around here to recover some gold he'd stolen?"

Willie and I looked at each other, "Yes, sir."

"Jack Lindstrom had a series of articles about it in the paper. Didn't give any names but it said that Romney shot a boy and held somebody hostage. He used them to get his gold as I understand. The wounded boy knew where it was and the other one had to go into a cave to recover it."

Buckley nodded, "That's right. Then what was it, he busted out of jail and was killed? My, my ... happened right around here, did it?"

"Yes, sir," Willie answered.

"How about that," Sherman said, "You know all about that. Well, I suppose you would since it happened around here."

"You could say that."

Buckley took out a pipe and pouch of tobacco. He blew through the pipe and tapped it on his heel. "I suppose you know the kids, too."

"Yeah, they live around here," Willie replied.

I guess we'd answered so many questions about the 'Romney incident' that opening up another discussion was the last thing either one of us wanted to do.

Neither of us had a watch, but I knew we were running behind, "I'm sorry, sir, but we both have chores to do."

"No, no, I'm sorry we kept you." Mr. Buckley responded, "If you ever run into a fellow by the name of Albert Barnum, give him my regards. You see, I was a detective in Chicago when he caught the Romney gang up here."

"He's my granddad!" I exclaimed. "I'd tell him today except he's up north on a fishing trip. They don't have electricity or a telephone at the cabin, but I'll tell him when he gets home on Sunday."

We exchanged goodbyes and started back down the dusty gravel road. We heard their car's engine roar to life and fade away. But soon afterward we heard another engine and stepped aside as a black pick-up passed us. There were words on the door that said 'Porter Construction Company" in bold white letters. Andy was riding in the back. They sped past us without incident or acknowledgment of our presence.

"Willie," I began, "what exactly are you up to with Andy Porter?"

Oh I knew what he'd told me before, but now I was intrigued by his interaction with Andy since the fight the previous day. And this was why I wanted to be alone with him. I wanted some answers without the distractions my siblings might cause.

He answered easily, "I think I'm getting somewhere with him, Hildi. I'm praying for him like the Bible says, '... pray for your enemies ... bless those who curse you. Bless and do not curse ...' I just wish he hadn't attacked Johnny."

"Why?"

"Because I've been working real hard not to give him a reason to fight me. And I've been trying not to return evil for evil. But when he lit into Johnny, well, I had to do something. Johnny mighta got hurt."

"You don't know that," I disagreed. "You didn't give Johnny the chance to try to defend himself. He might have *needed* to know that he *can* stand up to Andy."

He walked along silently. I supposed that he was chewing on this possibility.

"I never thought of that," he said finally.

"That's all right," I said, "You've made bigger mistakes when you didn't think something through!"

I gave his shoulder a playful shove and he responded in kind.

"So, here I am, trying to be more like Jesus, trying hard not to return evil for evil, and in trying to defend someone who I think is defenseless, I could end up making him think that he can't fight his own fights?"

I looked at the ground as I nodded my affirmation then asked, "You're really praying for Andy?"

"Especially last night. Those Porter brothers ... I think Andy learned how to be a bully from them. Maybe they torment him. Maybe his folks are the same way."

"You think Andy needs the Lord? How are you going to bring that up?" I guess I sounded sarcastic because Willie's reply was heated.

"Hildi, everyone needs the Lord! As far as bringing that up, I don't know ... but if I let the Lord lead me, He'll give me the words. And maybe it means being an example in all sorts of circumstances. Maybe it means suffering and not cursing when somebody wrongs me. Maybe it means taking a stand in love and not in hate."

I thought of the Scripture about Jesus' crucifixion "... like a sheep led to the slaughter He did not open His mouth ..." I quoted what I could remember. "Is that why you didn't say anything when Mr. Arnold beat you?"

He nodded.

"But Willie, you're not Jesus!"

Perhaps it was because I liked him differently now. But if we had been discussing this in Sunday school, I would have reacted in a whole different way.

"You surprise me." He said, sounding disappointed.

We both stopped and turned to each other. "Hildi, it's more than a label!"

He looked like he was searching for something in his mind, found it, and then continued, "Calling yourself a farmer doesn't make you a farmer! When a cow goes down in a boggy pasture and can't get up, a real farmer, the owner, goes out there, gets covered in mud and manure, struggles and strains, risking his own life to save that animal. He doesn't think about how bad he's going to smell getting covered in muck. He doesn't think about how dirty his clothes will get. His goal is to save that cow."

I pictured this very clearly in my mind because I'd experienced it. But I didn't make the connection.

"Say what you mean." I stated.

Willie seemed exasperated, "Being a 'Christian' *is* 'being Jesus', not just wearing a label."

He stared into my eyes, allowing the statement to sink in and leave a dent in my soul.

"That's hard, Willie," I finally said.

"But isn't it right?" he insisted. "It's easy to say you're a Christian, maybe harder to step up in front of a bunch of people and confess you're a sinner, maybe harder to be baptized, but then to live out your life like Jesus did ... yeah, you're right. It's hard!"

I was ashamed. Willie's faith in God had grown by leaps while mine seemed to have shrunk. Six months ago I had been the one reminding *him* of God's power and now *he* was teaching *me*!

"You've become so strong, I mean, stronger as a Christian than you were. What changed?" I knew it wasn't me.

"Nothing ... and everything." We started walking again, "What we've been through, the two of us ... hearing old Charlie Kiley pleading with Emmit Romney to repent and Romney choosing hell over salvation."

He glanced over at me, "... and there's you."

"Me?" I cried.

"You constantly point me back to the Lord, call me out when I do something stupid, remind me to pray for God's will and guidance instead of trying to do things my way."

I didn't know what to say. As I listened to Willie, I felt like a phony, like a fake. I couldn't see how I could have helped Willie's faith grow to this point. I didn't know whether to argue or be humbled.

Chapter Sixteen

We were nearly to the old town road, the sun was sitting a bit lower in the sky. After talking with the fishermen, we were about half an hour behind schedule.

"You think we ought to cut up the old town road?" I asked.

"Probably should."

But as we approached the little clearing in the woods where the old town road began, we saw a vehicle. It was the Porter Construction truck that had passed us earlier and it was parked on the old town road. All three brothers sat in the back, the two older boys on the tailgate and Andy on the side of the box. Sam, the oldest, puffed on a cigarette.

"Well, hello," called Sam.

I looked at Willie, "What do we do?"

"We can't go that way now. Just keep walking."

But as we began to pass, both older boys jumped down off the truck and cut us off.

"You're kind of unfriendly today" said Gabe. They weren't drunk this time.

"I apologize," Willie offered. "We've got chores to do and can't stop to talk."

Sam stepped uncomfortably close to us. He blew smoke into Willie's face as he spoke, "That a fact? Well, you've also got some unfinished business here that needs to be taken care of."

Sam dropped the cigarette onto the road and ground it out with his heel.

"That's right," added Gabe. "You marred our little brother's face. Now, yesterday, that little boy that was with you said you beat up Andy Porter. You said you didn't get to finish the fight. When we got home and saw our little brother over there, we decided we're gonna see that fight gets finished."

There was no fear in Willie's voice or his face as he responded, "I shouldn't have said that."

"That right? I'm lookin' at Andy right now and he's downright ugly with that black eye, swelled up nose, and split lip. Tell you what, you and Andy are gonna finish that fight right now. How's that?"

Willie looked him in the eye, "I'm not gonna fight him."

Sam waved Andy over. Andy didn't seem as excited about this as his brothers. He trudged over to where we were standing.

"Anybody coming down the road will see us," he complained.

"Then let's get off the road." Sam ordered.

Willie and I didn't move to follow them. Instead, we started down the road again only to be stopped a second time.

"I can't believe anybody who bragged about beating my brother would be chicken enough to run away from a fight."

"I'm walking away, not running," was Willie's response.

"No, you're not!" Sam grabbed Willie and spun him back towards the town road.

I stood there, trying to figure out what to do, when Andy pointed at me, "She'll run home and tell!"

And that's when Gabe approached me. The fact is that I wouldn't have run home. I was ready to take on the Porters alone if I had to, but now I followed Willie to a place beyond the truck where the ground was somewhat flat and the trees secluded us from the road.

Sam gave Willie a hard push, sending him sprawling.

"All right, Andy. He's all yours," he encouraged.

Andy slowly walked up to Willie, "You gonna fight me or not?"

"Not," he answered, picking himself up off the ground.

Andy turned, "He's not gonna fight."

"So?" exclaimed Gabe, "Hit him!"

Andy marched right up to Willie and balled up his fist, but Willie looked him in the eye. It wasn't a challenge. He didn't smile. He just waited.

"Come on, Cooper! Do something!" yelled Andy in his face.

"Hit him!" ordered Sam.

"He won't fight back!" screeched Andy pathetically.

Sam was on him in an instant, "How do you know he won't. You're both standing there like a couple of dummies!" Sam suddenly had a change of expression, "Or is it that you're afraid of him?"

Andy's eyes narrowed, "What? Why would you say that? I'm not afraid of him. Just look at him. I'm bigger! I'm stronger!"

"Then prove it!" yelled Gabe as he pulled a full pint bottle of whiskey from his rear pocket, opened it, and took a swallow.

He passed the bottle to his brother who also took a long drink. He then passed it to Andy who shook his head.

"You are turning into a regular choir boy, you know that?" Sam shook his head in disgust, and then turned to Willie.

"What about you? You need a little courage in a bottle?"

Willie held his ground, "I don't need that kind of courage."

Sam handed the bottle back to Gabe and I could see that he'd taken Willie's comment hard.

Suddenly, he clutched Willie's shoulder and punched him in the stomach. Willie's knees buckled and he went down, gasping for air.

"You want us to soften him up, maybe? Come here, Gabe. Hold him!"

Gabe pulled Willie up and held him by the arms. Sam hit him again and I could hear the breath escape in a grunt. His legs gave out and his face contorted as he tried to breathe.

"Leave him alone!" I yelled and made a move towards them.

Sam turned quickly, stepping in front of me, "You his sister?"

"No." I answered, glaring, desperately trying to get around him. I wanted to help my friend but Sam wouldn't let me pass. Suddenly, he seized me and passed me to Andy.

"Keep her back."

Gabe pulled Willie up as Sam landed a third blow.

But Andy didn't even try to keep me back. I ran at Gabe and hit him until he let go of Willie who made no effort to recover his footing. He writhed on the ground, coughing. Gabe took me by the arms and held me tight. Sam followed up the punch with a hard kick to Willie's ribs, sending him rolling into the leaves.

"There you go, little brother. You should be able to take him now."

But Andy just stood there with that same horrified look he'd had the day before after witnessing Mr. Arnold's brand of punishment.

"Well, come on! Get to it!" screamed Gabe over my head.

"He won't fight. Let's just go home!" Andy pleaded.

That's when Sam whirled on Andy. He took his shirt front in both hands and nearly lifted him off the ground, "You are not *'even' yet*! As soon as that kid catches his breath, he will be up strutting around like before! You said he's the big 'cock of the walk' at school. You said he's 'mister high and mighty.' And now it's your chance to show him who the bigger man is. By all the looks of it, it's him. He doesn't have a busted up face!"

Sam released his brother and backed away.

"Gimme that bottle, Gabe." Gabe gripped my arm in one hand and reached in his hip pocket with the other, retrieving the liquor and passing it to Sam who took a big swallow.

He swirled the amber liquid around. I looked down at Willie who seemed to be collecting himself. At least, he was on his hands and knees. He'd gotten his wind back and had stopped coughing. Andy took a step towards us. But then I felt Sam's eyes on me.

"How old are you?" He asked and his tone changed.

"Why does it matter?" I was suddenly uneasy. There was a familiarity in how Sam looked at me that I remembered from a night only a few months earlier.

He suddenly took me by both arms and pulled me out of Gabe's grip, "You know, you have really pretty hair, all long and wavy. You like to dance?"

I tried to get free, I twisted my body and tried to kick, but just when I thought I might gain purchase, he spun me towards his brother who caught me and pulled me tight against his chest. "What're you doin' with that scrawny boy?"

"Let go of me!" I screamed in anger. He spun me back to Sam who caught me around the waist and held me tight while he swayed.

That got Willie to his feet and he faced both Gabe and Sam, "Let her go!"

"Gabe, give Andy a drink."

"I told you I don't want any!" he shouted.

"Yes you do and you'll take a big drink if you know what's good for you! Porters get even. They settle the score!"

Gabe forced the bottle to Andy's lips. The boy's eyes narrowed as he looked from one brother to the other and then took the bottle in his own hands. He drank a long drink and handed it back to Gabe.

"There! You happy?" He bellowed.

"No. He's standing and there's not a mark on him!"

Willie was up but bent over with his hands on his knees, watching the exchange between the Porters. Andy looked spitefully at his brother and then at his 'opponent'. He opened his mouth and let out a roar as he charged Willie who deftly stepped back out of the way. Andy tripped and fell into the leaves, rolled over, and was back up in an instant.

"All right, Cooper! I've given you the chance to defend yourself! Now I'm coming and I don't care if you fight back or not!"

Willie stood his ground without flinching. Andy charged again, and again Willie sidestepped, but this time Andy didn't trip although he was slightly unsteady.

"Tell him to quit moving around!" Andy hollered.

"Quit movin' around!" laughed Gabe.

Sam still held me but was losing patience, "Hold onto her!"

Gabe took hold of me and held me tightly against his chest. The only thing I could move was my head and my feet which I tried to kick behind me without hitting anything.

Sam stalked towards Willie who didn't see him coming. He swung hard, landing a blow to the side of Willie's head and sending him to the ground, stunned.

"We've wasted too much time!" Sam hauled Willie up. He was limp, so Sam shook him, "C'mon, wake up."

Willie shook his head but he was still dazed.

"Hit him, Andy!"

Now clearly under the influence of the whiskey, Andy strode boldly up to Willie and pummeled him. It didn't last long, less than a minute. But in that time, he appeared to do more than enough damage to make up for what Willie had done to him. Sam let him fall to the ground and Gabe turned me loose. But instead of running to my friend, I went on the attack.

"You monsters!" I swung at Gabe and hit him in the mouth, cutting my knuckles. He swung at me but didn't connect. I tripped over my own feet and landed on my backside.

"Let's get outa here," Sam said blandly. "I'm hungry."

The truck roared to life and spun backward towards the road.

Willie lay face down in the leaves.

"Willie! Willie!"

I gently turned him over and heard him groan, "Oh!" He held his belly and turned onto his side.

"Willie!" I ordered, "Willie, look at me!"

He turned over on his back, trying to sit up and coughing, "Oh God, help me," he gasped.

"What is it? What can I do?" I begged.

"Can't breathe ..." he managed.

I remembered something daddy had done once when Joe had punched Ben in the stomach and knocked the wind out of him. I stood up, reached down and grabbed Willie's belt and pulled up on it, lifting him so that his back came up off the ground. I let him down and did it again. He seemed to settle down. I repeated the procedure and, although he groaned again, he was breathing easier.

He lay flat on his back with his knees bent and his eyes closed. I knelt down beside him and surveyed the damage done by Andy and his brothers. He had sustained bruises to his cheek and jaw. A trickle of blood oozed from the corner of his mouth and I dabbed at it with my shirt sleeve. When I did, I noticed my own injury. The cut on my hand was bleeding but I would have to deal with that later.

"Willie?" I said softly. No response.

"Will?" I tried.

"Uh," he moaned and opened his eyes.

"Willie?" I said again.

He took a deep breath and caught it, "I think he cracked a rib ... hurts when I take a deep breath."

"I'll get you home." I said firmly. "Sit up."

I eased him into a sitting position. The sun was much lower. I figured they would be looking for us at home. Getting there would not be easy. The old town road went up and over the bluff. That would be too difficult, so we would have to stay on the gravel road.

"Hildi," he said, "I think I'm getting somewhere with Andy."

"That's what you're thinking about? You are nuts!" I exclaimed.

He chuckled, "You know I'm right. He wasn't going to fight."

"I know. Here, put your arm around me. I'll help you stand up."

But he insisted on making his point, "He pulled his punches."

I stared at him a moment, "You'd never know it from the way you look!"

It was a feat to get Willie up and when I did, he leaned on me heavily.

"Do you think your ribs are broke? You've got blood in your mouth. Are you bleeding inside?"

"I bit my tongue. I'm not coughing blood. I don't know how to tell if a rib is broke or cracked. I'm just guessing. It hurts on one side."

We started walking, "I'm sorry for all the questions."

I pulled his arm around my neck and mine around his waist. We moved a little easier that way and made it to the road.

"I need a rest." He said.

"So soon?"

"Yeah."

"Do you want to sit?"

"No, just let me lean on you for a minute."

I did. We stood on the side of the road. His breaths came in short gasps and even though he wasn't big, he was becoming heavy. I thought about him and the girl in Montana. Maybe, if I got him talking, it would take his mind off his injuries and we could keep walking.

"Tell me again about Ramona Rawlins and the day the horse threw her."

I eased him into a slow walk, "We were ... riding along a mountain trail ... in the Bitterroots. She was ahead of me."

"What kind of a day?"

"Hot. Hot day with a hazy sky ... horse bolted ... she told me it reared ... a cougar spooked it ... horse threw her."

His sentences were broken, but he continued, "She's a good rider ... I'd seen her sit a bucking horse ... she stayed on good as any man ... couldn't believe it when I found her ..." He attempted a laugh.

"What did you do?"

"Gotta stop." He gasped.

"Do you need to sit down?"

"Yeah."

I kept my arm around him and lowered both of us to the roadside, "What did you do when you found her."

"Tried to wake her up. Checked for blood or a bump ... wasn't any. So, I kind of ... did what you're doin'... as long as I could. Finally ... I couldn't carry 'er any more. Got her to ... wake up and put her on ... my horse ..."

"Did you walk the horse or ride it?"

"Rode behind her ... had to hold onto her so she ... wouldn't slip off. When we got down ...

she kinda came too ... and she kissed me ... she *really* kissed me."

I wished we had a horse! What was that? She did what? He said it so easily!

"How did you know she was really hurt? I mean ... maybe she wasn't! You didn't actually see her fall ..."

He leaned against me again and shut his eyes, "Hildi?"

"What is it?"

"I liked it when you called me Will ... so soft and gentle ..."

"What?"

He sat up and looked at me with clear and alert eyes, "I said I liked it when you called me Will!"

He stood up on his own and looked down at me while holding out his hand.

"You liar!" I yelled, slapped his hand away and gave him a shove when I stood up, "There's nothing wrong with you!"

"Ow!" he cried, "Take it easy! My side really does hurt!"

But I wasn't listening, "How can you worry me like that? After everything we've been through! I oughta belt you!"

I stomped on ahead, irritated at the ruse. We were only a mile from home, but I heard the hum of an engine. It was coming the opposite direction from where the Porters had gone. I got off the road and waited. As it approached, it slowed down. I recognized Betty Cooper right away. When she saw me she pulled off the road.

"Hildi! Have you seen Willie? He's not home yet and I'm worried something's happened to him."

I turned and pointed behind me, "There he is!"

She got out of the car and ran to her brother.

"Where have you been?"

"We got sidetracked ..." I started to explain, but Willie cut me off.

"... by a couple of fishermen down in Ottertail creek. We got to talking and lost track of time."

But it was light enough for Betty to notice the bruises beginning to form on Willie's face. "So you had a fight with a couple of fishermen? Don't lie to me, Willie! Tell me what happened!"

Willie looked away, "They were waiting for me ... Sam, Gabe, and Andy."

"When we get home we're telling Ma! The Porters don't lose fights and they don't let other people make them look bad. I know Sam and Gabe Porter better than you!" Betty turned to walk away, but Willie caught her by the arm.

"No, Betty. I don't want her to make a fuss. Besides, it's not that bad."

"Really? Really, Willie? Go look in the mirror!"

I interrupted, "He looks better than Andy, a lot better. They think they've won. Why not leave it there?"

She crossed her arms and glared at him. "This isn't right, you know. I don't care that you've made Andy Porter your 'missionary project'. You're my little brother and look at you!"

Betty had tears in her eyes and struggled to keep her composure. "Just look at you! Your back is covered with welts from a crazy man; your face is bruised from the school yard bully! What's next, Willie? What's next? Am I going to find you lying dead in a ditch some day?"

When she began to sob, he looked lost, like he wasn't sure what to do. I felt like I was intruding because I just stood there. I didn't know if I should stay or go on down the road. He reached in his pocket and pulled out a bandana.

"I'm sorry," he said as he held it out to her. "I can't help it."

She took it and then pulled him to herself and held him tightly while she continued to cry. From the look on his face I could tell that she had no idea how her embrace must have hurt him. But, he didn't say anything to let her know.

Finally, when her shoulders stopped heaving, but as she continued to hold him, she spoke in a voice choked with emotion. "I know you think you have to do this. But, Willie, we've come so close to losing you ... you and Hildi ... more than once. We love you both and we want you to be safe!"

Willie had been standing like a little boy with his hands at his sides, but after those words, he returned her embrace. I left them there and went on home.

Chapter 17

I wasn't as late as I thought I would be. Honey and Queenie met me as I neared the barn. The cows were inside and Lila had just finished putting the milkers together. Mom was heading to the barn just as I approached the porch. She wore a scarf on her head and her brown corduroy barn coat. She also carried the two quart stainless steel pail to put milk in for our use. I bent to pet the dogs who 'washed my face' in appreciation.

"Where have you been?" she asked. "You're pretty late in getting home."

I didn't know if I should tell her the whole story or not.

"There were a couple of fishermen in the Ottertail and Willie and I stopped and gave them directions to Amundson's Fish Market. We were gonna come right home after that but we ran into the Porter brothers and Willie had some trouble."

"What kind of trouble? Is he hurt? Are you hurt?" She noticed the cut on my hand and reached for it.

"I cut it on Gabe's tooth. They wanted him to fight, but he wouldn't. So Andy's brothers tried to force him to fight." I didn't tell her everything.

She pursed her lips and her eyes narrowed, "I don't like this. I don't like this one bit!"

"Mom, it should be over now. They just wanted to get even."

"Getting even!" she exclaimed, "If anyone should understand the harm of revenge it should be you and Willie! Every time I hear about 'getting even', a child gets hurt. I'm going to call Julia. If it has come to the point where you can't even walk home from school without being threatened, then it has gone too far."

"But, Mom ..."

She held up a hand, "Go wash that cut good and put some iodine on it. Then you'd better change your clothes and go out to the barn. You've got chores to do."

Mom turned and went back inside the house with me following. I knew that the call to Willie's mom would not have pleasant outcomes for Willie. I also knew that what would most likely follow would be a trip to see the Porters with Willie in tow to provide evidence of the beating he'd just suffered at the hands of the brothers. And I knew he would most likely be upset with me for 'spilling the beans.'

I could hear her placing the call as I changed into my barn clothes. I didn't want to hear it, didn't want to be responsible for the call. You see, we had an unwritten code in our 'kid kingdom': Fight your own battles. Any kid who had his parents intervene was considered a coward and was looked down upon by the others. However, we'd never, ever had anything like this happen before and the last person to have anyone fight his battles was Willie! Nevertheless, I wouldn't know the outcome of the call because when Mom hung up the telephone, she headed down the road in our truck. I knew she was going to the Coopers' house.

When I got to the barn, I informed the others of what was going on.

"It's about time!" exclaimed Ben.

We were astonished and he picked up on our surprise right away. "Well, you guys weren't on the other end of it! Maybe those Porters will move back to town where they belong!"

We waited a little for Mom to get back, but when she didn't, we did the milking alone. We finished our chores, turned the cattle out, and fixed our own supper. Then we did something we wouldn't have done if she had been home: we let the dogs inside.

It was around 7:30 when the truck returned. We all sat around the kitchen table doing our homework when she walked in the back door.

"Why are the dogs in the house?" She sounded a bit cross.

Queenie was lying under the table while Honey sat on Lila's lap.

"They're not doing anything. Can't they please stay in a little longer?" Joe pleaded.

She looked at both dogs, cocked her head, and smiled. "All right. Ten minutes."

We all looked at her in hopes that she would share what happened.

"Did you get the cows all milked?" she asked while taking off her coat.

"Yes," Lila answered for all of us. "Are you gonna tell us about it?"

Mom went to the sink and began running water to wash dishes. She had a terse smile and shook her head but it didn't mean 'no'. It was her way of conceding.

"Elaine Porter is a good woman caught between a rock and a hard place. Her sons are wild and her husband encourages them to be that way. Any time she tries to set them straight or teach them any discipline, he overrules her." Thus began her narrative. She talked as she washed the dishes.

"We took Willie and went to see her. The boys weren't around and she invited us in. Apparently this isn't the first time she's had this kind of a 'visit'. So, she put on a pot of coffee and we talked. We had planned to leave Willie in the car unless someone wanted proof of what had been done to him. But she asked us to take him inside so she could have a look at him. It turns out that she's a nurse and works part time at the hospital in Ridgeview. If she hadn't insisted on seeing Willie, Julia never would have seen the extent of the beating he'd gotten from Mr. Arnold. Mrs. Porter was clearly upset when she saw his back and the bruises on his face, but when she felt his ribs and found one broken and another possibly cracked, she just broke down. 'My boys did this!' she kept saying over and over. When she finally pulled herself together, she got some bandages and wrapped his ribs up tight and put iodine on his back.

"What should have been about a fifteen-minute confrontation turned into an hour and a half heart-to-heart talk between three moms. Willie told her the boys had been drinking. Apparently, they've been stealing whiskey from their father' liquor cabinet.

"She told us they keep moving because of her husband's construction jobs, but it's more likely on account of the problems the boys cause. She doesn't know how long they'll be in the area now that Dobkins has stopped work on the Crenshaw house. Her husband started another project on the other side of the state and is gone all week. That right there can be a reason for the boys running wild. But we got a sample of what he's like because we were there when he came home.

"That man! As soon as he learned who we were, he began swearing about the beating *Willie* had given *Andy*. She did her best to calm him down, but he just became more irritated, so we left.

"I really feel sorry for that woman. It's obvious to me that the boys take after their daddy and that the idea of 'getting even' comes from him. He carried in a case of beer and had already been at it when he walked in the door."

Mom joined us at the kitchen table.

"We invited her to come to church with us, even offered to go get her. She hasn't been to church in years, husband won't allow it. I can't imagine your daddy keeping me out of the Lord's house. She is a Christian woman, but she was blinded by love and married a man who doesn't know the Lord ... like I said, between a rock and a hard place."

Chapter Eighteen

ALL NIGHT TEEN SKATE!
October 24-25,
8:00 p.m. to 7:00 a.m.

I read the poster on the door of Anderson's general store in Cedar Grove. Anderson's was great! Not only did it carry canned foods, but there were fabric and sewing notions in an upstairs balcony area where you could go and pick out patterns, too. I mostly wanted to go up there so I could look down on the entire store. There were oil lamps, wicks and chimneys; pots, pans and dishes; hardware as well as smoked meats.

Daddy was across the street talking to Lyle Gander, the owner of the local garage, while he changed our sparkplugs. It had been a week since my mom and Willie's mom had gone to see Mrs. Porter. I wondered if she had done something to make a difference because Andy seemed a little different. He wasn't as quick to cause trouble, not that he had changed completely, far from it. But we all seemed to be getting along. He even brought a football and took the time to tell us how the game was played. Willie couldn't participate due to his sore ribs, but maybe that was why Andy had changed. It puzzled me but I didn't waste any time trying to figure it out!

I had a short list of supplies to pick up for Mom.   The list included a box of matches, condensed milk, ten pounds of sugar, and coffee. I had just finished paying for the order and was on my way out the door when I noticed the poster and read it. The skating rink in Ridgeview had only been open a year but had grown in popularity. The many churches in the area had put together the outing that was being advertised on the poster. The event would happen next week, beginning Friday night at 8:00 and lasting until 7:00 Saturday morning. I didn't know if I wanted to go. I didn't like skating. I just wasn't coordinated. Lila, however, was a good skater. She was graceful and could even skate backwards. But she couldn't go because she was only twelve.

I was about to leave when the door opened and I was standing face-to-face, or rather face-to-chest, with a tall and very handsome blond-haired man, who looked to be at least Daddy's age. He smiled down at me as he held the door open and stepped back out of the way.

"Pardon me, Miss. Go ahead, I've got the door."

I returned his smile and said, "Thank you."

The sidewalks in Cedar Grove were elevated in front of the General store at least three and a half feet. Even though it would have been shorter for me to jump down and cross the road to the garage, I opted to walk to the end of the short block near the 'Day's Over' Tavern and cross there. The tavern didn't just sell liquor but was a restaurant, too. The smell of pancakes and bacon floated through the open door.

I was still smiling to myself after the encounter with the fellow at the store when a big fancy car pulled up to the curb and parked. Out stepped a fairly short and very fat man in a grey double-breasted suit. His fedora matched his suit perfectly. He glanced at me but didn't smile. He marched up the steps of the tavern and went inside.

"What are you all smiles about?" Daddy asked when I entered Gander's Garage.

"Oh, a man opened the door for me over at Anderson's. He called me 'Miss' and had a nice smile."

"Well isn't that *nice*," Lyle remarked as he used his ratchet to tighten the plug he was working on. "These plugs I took out were fouled, Matt. You might want to give this old truck a tune-up before winter."

Lyle spewed a stream of dark tobacco juice towards a drain in the floor. The area was stained darkly and I couldn't tell if it was from Lyle's spit or from oil.

"I know. Maybe we can bring 'er in for a tune up in a week or so. Right now I need it for hauling corn up to the mill."

We heard a commotion outside. There were raised voices and we turned towards the sound.

"What in blazes ..." Lyle exclaimed, but in a hoarse whisper. He looked at Daddy and both went for the door. I followed close behind.

Across the street I could see the tall man and the short fat man standing as close to nose-to-nose as two men of such differing stature could.

"I have men who haven't been paid! You owe me $700 for building supplies and the work we completed before you shut down the project!" the tall man bellowed.

"And I told you, your sons do not qualify as employees!" spat the shorter man.

"They know as much about tearing out walls as any man who's ever worked for me!"

"That doesn't prove anything! You let your men walk off the job! That's your problem! I'll pay for qualified workers, not *teen-age sons* of contractors!"

The tall man stepped back and sized up the other. Finally, he reached up and scratched his head, "I bet you don't have the money! Is that it, Dobkins? You don't have the money so you closed down the project? You don't have the money so you can't pay me what you owe!"

"Shut up, Porter, or I'll find another contractor!"

"Good luck finding someone who'll work for nothing!"

The argument ended when the shorter man turned on his heel and marched to his car. Dust and dirt flew as he spun out of town.

The tall man leaped down off the walk in front of the store and came our way. Did the other man call him 'Porter?' Was this Andy's father?

"Tough morning, Rueben?" asked Lyle when the man approached.

"Very tough, my friend." He replied and noticed me. "Well now, young lady, I see you've unloaded your package."

"Rueben, have you met Matt Barnum?"

The man smiled again and held out his hand, "Can't say that I have. I'm Rueben Porter."

Daddy gripped his hand and held it a moment, "The Crenshaw house?"

Porter nodded, "Yeah. That's me ... I guess you heard us."

Daddy nodded.

Rueben smiled and rubbed his chin. "So, are you in town for long? This your truck?"

"I needed new spark plugs," Daddy replied.

"How 'bout a beer? I'll buy," offered Rueben.

Daddy smiled, "No thanks. We're about done here and I need to pick up our feed."

"Another time then?" said Rueben.

I wondered how my father would respond. We didn't drink alcohol and Daddy didn't frequent the taverns in town. From what I had heard from Mom, Rueben Porter was a hard drinker and so were his boys.

"I'll tell you what," my father responded, "why don't you come out to our place for supper one night or maybe dinner after church tomorrow? Hildi and your boy go to school together and it would be nice to get to know your family."

Porter raised his eyebrows and smiled at me, "Church? We're not really 'church people.' Besides, I'm taking my older boys to the river tomorrow. But supper one night sounds like something we could do."

"Fine. We'll look forward to it."

Daddy placed his heavy hand on my shoulder and looked down at me. I wondered if he was reading my mind because I was thinking that *I* wouldn't be looking forward to supper with the Porters.

***

Once a week we would run to Cedar Grove for feed or fuel or groceries and one of us would get to go with Daddy alone. When I got to go, I felt like I could ask him questions I wouldn't dare ask if Mom was around. Or, just maybe, I could look a little harder at the people in town to see if I recognized a certain boy my age without my siblings being around to notice and tease. And that is exactly what I did as we drove up the winding road to the feed mill on the outskirts of town. I scanned the trucks that waited in line to either pick up feed they bought or, like us, have their corn ground into feed. Daddy parked our truck and I followed him inside to the counter. I'd hoped that maybe I'd see the Coopers. I knew that Saturdays they normally came to the mill for feed. But they weren't waiting in line at the counter and their truck wasn't parked outside, either.

The feed mill had an area where you made your orders for custom ground feed or you could buy fencing hardware or other farm supplies. It was a fairly gloomy place, quite dark with a lot of grain dust that covered everything. But I liked the way it smelled. I'd had my eye on a fancy leather calf halter and each time we went in, I went to see if anyone had bought it. I made my way there and wasn't surprised to see it still hanging on its peg. I reached up and touched the soft brown leather and ran my hand along the length of the lead line. It was connected to the halter by about six inches of brass chain. I imagined how it might look on one of our cows at the county fair.

"'Mornin,' Jiggs," I heard Daddy say to the man behind the counter.

"Hi, Matt. You gotta line ahead of you. It might be a while." Jiggs only had one hand. He'd lost the other during the 'Great War' or World War One. He used a hook-like apparatus to hold a clipboard still while he wrote Daddy's name on a list. He had a cigarette between his lips which he'd smoked down to the butt end.

"I saw that. I just wanted to pick up some insulators and gate hooks before we get in line."

The noise in this part of the mill was only half as loud as where the corn was being ground. Out there you had to shout to be heard. Inside, you just had to contend with a constant rumble. Even so, if you weren't paying attention, you wouldn't hear the door open or anyone talking to you unless they spoke up.

Daddy busied himself by opening boxes of white porcelain insulators and inspecting them to make sure there were no cracks or breaks. He wanted both insulators to nail to wooden posts and corner insulators for running wires around corners.

"I look at that halter every time I come in here, too," said the familiar voice.

I turned in delight to see Willie standing behind me. I hadn't heard him come in, much less walk up behind me.

"I wondered if I'd see you here!" I exclaimed with a bit too much enthusiasm, but he didn't seem to notice or be repelled by it.

Willie was back to wearing overalls. Every day in school he had worn dungarees but now he was back wearing what I had always seen him in before. I noticed a large envelope sticking out of the bib pocket. I could easily read the Montana postmark.

"You got a letter." I stated. "I suppose it's from Ramona?"

His mouth was a straight line and he rolled his eyes.

He took the letter out of his pocket and handed it to me unopened.

"What? You don't want me to read this."

"You might as well."

I tried to hand it back to him. "Willie, I'm not gonna read your letter."

But he backed away and held up his hands, "No, you go ahead and read it. It'll give you something to do while you wait."

I couldn't tell if he was angry with me or not, but I felt the weight of the letter and noticed the extra postage stamps that were attached. Ramona Rawlins had beautiful handwriting and had addressed the letter to Mr. William Cooper. 'William' sounded so grown up!

"Hildi," Daddy called. He held two boxes of insulators and three gate hooks in his hands.

"You gonna come and sit in the truck with me or wait around with him?" He didn't even glance at Willie. Chet had already left and was probably in line with his truck.

"I'll wait outside," I barely got the words out and he was gone.

"Come on," said Willie and I followed him to a loading dock on the other side of the mill.

We climbed up a steep embankment to get high enough to climb onto the loading dock. The big doors were shut, but there was still plenty of room to sit with our backs against the doors. We did that and let our legs dangle. It was quieter here.

I still held the sealed letter from Ramona Rawlins.

"Open it, Hildi."

"Willie, I don't wanna read your letter!"

He pointed to the envelope, "Open it."

I turned the envelope over, slipped my finger under the flap and tore it open. I looked at him and he nodded for me to go on.

"Willie, I don't want to read this just because you're mad that I noticed it."

The mill was on one side of a deep valley but high enough to see the farms on the hilltops three miles away. That was where he set his eyes, not looking at me, not looking at the letter, or the ground or anything.

"I'm not mad. And it's not all about you."

That caught me off guard and I didn't know what was meant by it.

"What do you ...?"

He cut me off, "Read the letter, Hildi."

I unfolded the pretty pink stationary carefully and a heavy silver identification bracelet fell out. She had wrapped several extra pieces of paper around it. I turned the bracelet in my hand and read the inscription, 'Billy Cooper'. I turned it over and engraved on the back was 'Love, Ramona.' Once again I felt the pang of jealousy and fought it as I handed it to Willie. He studied it briefly and then tucked it in the bib pocket of his overalls.

A stiff breeze caught the corners of the paper bending the pages over so I had to hold them tighter.

Dearest William (Billy),

Today is Wednesday and I am supposed to be reading my English assignment. It is so boring that I thought my time would be better spent writing to you. I miss you so much! I think your uncle Ethan misses you, too. You were such a big help. The barn was never cleaner than when you were here.

Daddy let me drive the Cadillac around the ranch. That was great fun until I discovered some lazy ranch hands taking a break. They said it was their lunchtime, but I told them if they didn't get back to work I would have them fired. You should have seen how quickly they went back to work! I will be getting my license next spring.

When I do, I can come and see you. Remember, I told you I would!

The Bitterroots are beautiful this time of year. We drove up to that diner in Stevensville that has the apple pie. Daddy can't understand why I'm ordering a slice of cheddar cheese with my pie now. It's all because of you!

The horses are not getting nearly as much exercise as when we worked them together. Daddy says I should be exercising the horses by myself. But I told him I just can't without someone with me. 'Your' mare, Osceola, is in foal. She is one nasty mama! She's been baring her teeth at the other brood mares and Ethan has to keep an eye on her or she may turn her heels at them. If she gets another horse cornered she'll kick it to death!

I often look at the pictures I took of us last summer and can't believe you were only here six weeks. To me, it seems like we've known each other all our lives. I know you are younger than I am, but there are other couples where the girl is older than the boy. And you never acted like a little boy, Billy. You are my Romeo!

At this point I had to stop. Partly because this letter was making me sick!

"Romeo? What does she mean you are her 'Romeo'? And what does she mean 'you never acted like a little boy'?"

He pointed to the letter, "Keep going. She's just warming up."

Romeo, Romeo! Wherefore art thou? Oh how I wish you were here!

'Good grief!' I thought.

Now, don't think I'm complaining. I know you are not big in the letter writing department. Maybe this is something you farm boys don't do. But I so want to hear from you. I need something from you to know you are still alive. I relive those rides we took. Especially, when you saved my life! A thousand kisses would never be enough to repay you! But I'm willing to try! Here is a little something I picked up in Missoula. I hope you will wear it.

So please, write back to me ... unless you are going to break my heart! Is there someone else? Because if there is, I will just die! I will! I will kill myself! Please, Please, Please Billy Boy! Write me and tell me you love me, too.

All my love,
Ramona

After her signature she had apparently put on too much red lipstick and kissed the paper.

I folded the letter and put it back in the envelope.

"Now do you see what I'm going through? Every Saturday ... and they're all mushy!"

"What did you do to this girl?" I exclaimed.

"Nothing. Why? Did she say she would die?" He flicked a stray pebble off the loading dock.

I handed him the letter, "She said she would kill herself!"

"Don't let it worry you. She loves *herself* more than anyone else!"

I shook my head. She called him 'Romeo' and I was pretty sure somebody killed herself in that story.

"I don't know," I said. "It sounds like she would die for you."

He returned the letter to its envelope and carelessly stuffed it in his pocket.

"That's a pretty serious statement. But I'm pretty sure she wouldn't die for me if she really had to make a choice like that."

I shrugged my shoulders, "Who could ever know if they would really die for someone else?"

But he turned slowly and looked at me hard, "I do ... and so do you."

The naked truth of his statement penetrated deep into my soul and I was ashamed that I had forgotten so easily. But now I remembered: he would have died for me ... twice.

We were frozen, our eyes locked, sitting close together in the chilly October air. My heart felt like it would burst through my chest. I felt like the world was spinning, maybe because I was holding my breath in anticipation as he slowly leaned towards me. I told myself to breath or I'd faint.

"Hey, you two!" hollered a voice and the spell was broken. Willie looked away first and motioned at our dads standing at the far corner of the mill.

"We're done! Let's go home!" Chet yelled, mostly because they stood at the noisy end of the feed mill.

Willie got up first and then reached down and helped me to my feet. We carefully navigated the steep embankment that led to the loading dock and walked casually the rest of the way.

"Did you see the poster for the all-night skate?" I asked him.

He winced, "You hate skating!"

"Yeah, but you're pretty good and it might be fun. Maybe you can teach me how to skate better."

He laughed, "I don't think I can teach you how to be less clumsy!"

We were both laughing when we got to the trucks. I climbed in and Daddy started the engine. I turned and waved out the back window as we pulled away.

He gave me a sideways look. "You happy about something?"

I couldn't help it. I knew I was grinning. "Maybe."

"Well, would you like to share? Or is this one of those moments only another female would understand?"

I looked at him. His eyes twinkled. I guess he knew more than I gave him credit for. He had been my age once, but I didn't know a lot about what Daddy was like then.

"I think it's a 'female' thing, Daddy."

He chuckled and turned his attention to the road.

Chapter Nineteen

"This will be our last lesson in this series about the love of Christ and how Christians are commanded to love." said Selma Potter as she looked around the table at us.

"Is that what we've been studying?" squawked George Lowry who was going through a serious voice change.

Mrs. Potter chuckled and Lila shook her head, "How can you not know that?"

As usual, the Coopers were late, so it was just George Lowry, Virginia Jessup, Lila, and me. We opened our Bibles as Selma gave us each a Scripture to look up and read.

"Oh my, I have run out of readers. I have two more scriptures ..."

We heard someone coming down the steps and waited for Willie. But when the curtain was pulled aside, instead of whom we expected, there stood Andy Porter and my father.

"Here you go, son. This is your class."

Andy looked around sheepishly. He was dressed up and had his hair combed, but unlike us, he didn't carry any Bible.

"Well good morning, young man," Selma Potter smiled and greeted him with genuine warmth. "And who are you?"

Daddy spoke up, "This is Andy Porter. They're renting the Oliver place down the road and it's his first time in Sunday school class."

Daddy gave me a look that Andy couldn't see and no one else but my sister would understand. The look told me that I was to be patient and give this fellow a chance, despite what I knew about him!

"Very good, Andy! Why don't you sit right there by Lila Barnum?"

He pulled out the wooden chair and sat beside her.

"We're looking up scriptures right now. Oh, you don't have a Bible. Just a minute …"

Along the wall and immediately under the steps was a short bookcase with two shelves on it. Among the few copies of old hymnals and commentaries were a some spare Bibles. They were not in the best shape as the basement had flooded two years earlier and some of the books had gotten wet. She found one that looked like the pages weren't sticking together with a pretty good binding and passed it down the table to our new student.

"There you go. I'm sure Lila will be happy to help you find your scripture and then when I call on you, you can read it."

For the first time since I'd known him, Andy looked uncomfortable.

"Your scripture is 1 Peter 2:21-24. Lila will help you find that." Mrs. Potter looked over a small sheet of lined paper on which she had written her notes for the class. She held her finger in one place and then checked a dainty watch on her thick wrist.

"I have one more verse here but I don't think anyone else is coming so I will have to find this one."

She opened her Bible, turned the pages, quickly finding the book, chapter and verse.

"Now, let's see … Virginia, you have Romans 12:9. Would you read that, please?"

"*Love without hypocrisy. Abhor what is evil; cling to what is good.*"

"George, now read Luke 6:35."

George held a card under the words as he read, "*But love your enemies, and do good, and lend, expecting nothing in return; and your reward will be great, and you will be sons of the Most High; for He Himself is kind to ungrateful and evil men."*

"Hilda, 1 Corinthians 13:1-8."

I was ready with the verses and my passage was the longest of all.

"If I speak with the tongues of men and of angels, but do not have love, I have become a noisy gong or a clanging symbol. And if I have the gift of prophecy, and know all mysteries and all knowledge; and if I have all faith, so as to remove mountains, but do not have love, I am nothing. And if I give all my possessions to feed the poor, and if I deliver my body to be burned, but do not have love, it profits me nothing. Love is patient, love is kind, and is not jealous; love does not brag and is not arrogant, does not act unbecomingly; it does not seek its own, is not provoked, does not take into account a wrong suffered, does not rejoice in unrighteousness, but rejoices with the truth; bears all things, believes all things, hopes all things, endures all things. Love never fails; but if there are gifts of prophecy, they will be done away; if there are tongues, they will cease; if there is knowledge it will be done away."

We heard someone coming down the steps, and in a moment the curtain was pulled back, and Willie stepped in.

"There you are!" exclaimed Selma, "Good. Sit down next to Hilda and look up 2 Corinthians 5:14. Where are we? Oh, Lila! You have Romans 12:19-21."

Lila had just finished showing Andy what he would be reading soon and I saw him following the words with his fingers.

"Never take your own revenge, beloved, but leave room for the wrath of God, for it is written, "Vengeance is Mine, I will repay," says the Lord. But if your enemy is hungry, feed him, and if he is thirsty, give him a drink; for in so doing you will heap burning coals upon his head. Do not be overcome by evil, but overcome evil with good."

"Andrew, you may read now." She directed.

Andy cleared his throat and read, *"For you have been called for this purpose, since Christ also suffered for you, leaving you an example for you to follow in His steps, who committed no sin, nor was any deceit found in His mouth; and while being reviled, he did not revile in return; while suffering, He uttered no threats, but kept entrusting Himself to Him who judges righteously; and He Himself bore our sins in His body on the cross, that we might die to sin and live to righteousness; for by His wounds you were healed."*

He looked up at her and she smiled her approval.

"And would you read the last Scripture, William?"

"For the love of Christ controls us, having concluded this, that one died for all, therefore all died; and He died for all that they who live should no longer live for themselves, but for Him who died and rose again on their behalf."

Selma looked around at us, "In the last five weeks we have read each of these verses and discussed them at length. I have one more passage that I will read for you. It is found in Romans 5:6-8. *For while we were still helpless at the right time Christ died for the ungodly. For one will hardly die for a righteous man; though perhaps for the good man someone would dare even to die. But God demonstrates his own love toward us, in that while we were yet sinners, Christ died for us.*

"In all of this discussion about love, Christ's love for the church, God's love for us by sending Jesus to pay the penalty for our sins, too often we sound like this loving is an easy thing. We certainly love other Christians. We love our family, even family members who are not

Christians. But this final verse drives home what should be different about the 'worldly' view of love and the Biblical view. That is, that we, Christians, are commanded to love even those who hate us. This isn't a wimpy thing, boys! It takes courage and strength not to strike back when someone insults us. It takes courage and strength not to hit someone who hits us first. And it's not enough to go through the motions. The verses in 1 Corinthians that Hilda read tell us that if you do all those things but lack love, it is useless. The Romans verses tell us to love without hypocrisy. Another passage says '... let love be genuine."

I watched Andy sit back and stare at the open book on the table. His eyes were narrowed but not in anger. He looked as though he was thinking hard. He turned suddenly and spoke up, "So what you're saying is that if you're a Christian, you can't fight back?"

Selma's warm smile crossed the table with her words, "What the Bible says is that Christians must have the love of Christ. That love, with the help of the Holy Spirit, helps us discern whether the fight is retaliation or a just cause. We just finished a war on two continents. I would say that those fights were just, wouldn't you?"

Andy nodded.

"But many of the things we go through on a daily basis turn into worthless battles. Fights I hear about are a person getting even for something done to him. In all reality, both parties can keep trying to get even until one of them takes the ultimate revenge and the other winds up dead. Oh, that might seem like an extreme, but not so long ago there were families who did just that. Those were called feuds. I think you might have heard of the Hatfields and the McCoys."

The time had flown for we soon heard the big church bell clanging overhead, signaling that it was time for worship.

"Now, before our closing prayer, I would remind you of the all-night teen skate in Ridgeview. The churches are sponsoring this and will be providing sandwiches, cakes, and punch, but we need to know if you are going, so we can get a rough estimate on how much to prepare. You don't have to stay all night if you don't want to. No one will lock you in or lock you out. But you do have to be at least thirteen to attend, so that leaves a few of you out. Andy, you would be welcome to go, too."

***

I suppose I shouldn't have been surprised when Mom invited the Porters to sit with us during church. Andy's mom brought her own Bible and followed along as Pastor Potter preached. I tried not to stare, but I wanted to get Andy's reaction to this 'religious' stuff. Maybe it was being in a new environment. Maybe it had something to do with not being able to be the center of attention, but Andy listened, sometimes intently, leaning forward and looking hard at the preacher.

Following the service everyone wanted to meet the Porters. People in our area were farm folks and were lucky to get out once a week to go to town. It was rare to meet new people, and when the opportunity to meet someone new came up, folks seized upon it. Andy disappeared and I scanned the church building to see where he was.

I glanced out the window and saw Willie and him standing along the road. Neither one of them looked agitated, but still, I wondered what would have drawn them together. I couldn't believe that the Lord had changed Andy's heart that fast. I decided not to intrude, found my folks, and headed home.

Chapter Twenty

"Are you going?" Barb Bjornstad didn't go to our church, but she still planned on attending the skating party.

"I suppose," was my answer. I still wasn't excited about roller-skating, but I had another reason to go.

Barb and a few of us girls had opted to stay inside. There was a cold north wind running through the valley. The boys went outside because Andy had brought his football again and wanted to start a game. Willie was determined to play even though his rib was not yet mended.

"You know, my folks think something is going to happen that night," Barb said with a sense of conspiracy.

Stella Johnson rarely sat with us, but today she did. "Like what?"

Barb leaned in, "The night of the skating party is the anniversary of August Crenshaw's suicide! He hung himself right from the banister!"

This drew the attention of even Miss Hendricks who seemed to cock an ear towards us.

"They are saying that the town is on edge. The kids in the high school are wound up; more fighting in the taverns; the telephone lines going dead, and the electricity fading down. There are a lot of weird things happening in that town."

Of course, we hadn't heard any of this except for the fights in the taverns which weren't anything unusual in Ridgeview.

"Really?" Lila asked.

"Sure!" she answered, "My big brother told me about it."

Well, if my aunt Ruth was the gossip in our family, Barb was the gossip in our little school. I listened to everything she said and believed less than half of it.

"Something's gonna happen at midnight 'cause that's when he died--at the stroke of midnight!"

I shook my head. Details like dates and times always stuck with me. "That's not right.

August Crenshaw died between 1:00 and 1:14 in the morning."

Barb was taken aback. I wasn't trying to insult her, but I had. She rolled her eyes and tossed her head.

"Hildi Barnum, you just think you know everything!"

But surprisingly, Stella came to my defense. "She does this time. I read about it last month. The paper re-printed the story from fifty years ago and it said that August Crenshaw had been coming and going from the upstairs balcony and threatened to shoot anyone who came in the door. He had barricaded the back door so they couldn't get in that way. Around 1:15 they didn't see or hear him and figured that maybe he had escaped. They broke down the door, to find him hanging from the railing of the second floor stairway."

Barb sniffed, "Doesn't matter. What *does* matter is that everything points to something happening that night! And I want to be close when it happens!"

I'd had enough. I didn't care about the cold wind outside, so I left.

Our open playground worked pretty well as a baseball field and now as a football field. We didn't have any yard lines, but the boys had set out some big rocks to mark goal lines. I watched as they tried to move the ball towards one of them. They didn't have any equipment but tackled each other with gusto. When I went out, they had just piled onto some unlucky fellow and were slow on getting off him.

"Let's go boys!" yelled Andy, and I noticed one of my brothers on his side while the other was on the opposite.

Finally, the last couple of boys climbed off their victim. I wasn't surprised to see it was Willie. He was slow in getting up but wasn't about to quit.

"I'm sorry, Willie, I just couldn't get open," Johnny Iverson apologized.

"That's ok. Forget it."

I reasoned that Willie tried to pass to Johnny but couldn't get rid of the ball before Andy's side tackled him.

I sat by the pump and watched. This was not any kind of a well-trained team. There were no assigned positions, just a kid on each side who tried to throw the ball to another kid who tried to run it into the make-shift end zone. Willie was serving in this capacity on one side but without much success. Once again the boys set up their lines of scrimmage. Willie yelled out random numbers that had no meaning and got ready to toss the ball to someone on his own team. He stepped back and let fly straight at my brother

Ben, but Andy jumped in, intercepted, and ran to the opposite end of the playground.

"Touch down! Ha! That makes the score twenty one to nothing!" yelled Norm, "C'mon! Let's go again!"

Everyone was red-faced and sweaty despite the forty-degree temperature and the cold wind. I knew the schoolhouse would be quite aromatic the rest of the day thanks to this football game. Despite the loss, most of the boys looked happy and enthusiastic. Johnny looked exhausted and his glasses were fogged up. Willie was bent over, catching his breath.

"C'mon, Andy!" urged Norm. "Cooper! Let's go, we've got time. Let's keep playing!"

Andy looked at Willie who finally straightened up and limped back to what would have been the scrimmage line.

"No." Andy said, "I've had enough. Let's cool off and go in."

Norm wanted to argue, but Andy brushed him off. When the other boys saw that the game was done, they walked or jogged back to the schoolhouse. Andy stood back a moment as the others passed him on the way to the pump. I got out of the way while they took turns pumping and drinking from the gush of cold water that came from the spout.   That was when I caught a glimpse of wonder. Andy walked right up to Willie.

"You play hard, Cooper."

Willie didn't say anything, only followed him back to the pump. Joe saw me standing nearby. His shirtsleeves were rolled up and there was a big bloody scrape on his forearm.

"Did you see us, Hildi?"

I nodded, "Looks kind of dangerous."

I indicated his arm.

He shrugged. "This? It's nothing!"

I went back up the stairs and inside to the warmth of the room.

The boys soon followed and the place was filled with chatter. We still had ten minutes left of our noon hour, but the look Miss Hendricks gave told us we might not if we didn't quiet down.

Willie went to his desk and sat. I noticed him grimace when he did. The desk in front of him was empty, so I went to it, "You ok?"

He nodded, but he held his side.

I knew better than to disagree with him or scold him. He didn't need another 'mom', but I knew if Lila had seen him that would be exactly what he'd have.

I went back to my own desk and pulled out the homework that had been assigned for the afternoon classes.

"Cooper," Andy sat down behind Willie, "you going to that roller-skating thing?"

"Yeah. My pa's gonna take a carload. Did you want to go? I think we've got room for one more."

Andy held up a hand, "Naw. My brothers are looking for an excuse to go to Ridgeview. If I go, they'll take me."

Then he lowered his voice. "Fact is, Cooper, my brothers think more of you than they do of me. That's part of the reason my pop wouldn't take me with him on Sunday. That's why my mom drug me to church. They're calling me a coward and now I gotta prove 'em wrong!"

"How?" Willie whispered back.

I listened intently.

"The Crenshaw house. It's locked up but Sam said he can get the key. They want me to spend a night in the Crenshaw house ... that night ... the night of the anniversary of Crenshaw's suicide, the same night as that roller skating thing."

"Why tell me?"

"I've heard things about you ... I've watched you. You're different. Maybe ... maybe you could pray for me?"

"But, it's just a night."

"Yeah ... just a night. Forget it, Cooper."

Andy looked embarrassed and turned his face away. But Willie encouraged him.

"No. It's ok. I'll do it. I'll pray for you."

After school we walked rapidly along the road, the wind blowing and our ungloved hands growing numb.

"So," after eavesdropping on Willie and Andy's conversation, I wanted to know who was included in this 'car load' he'd mentioned. "Are you going Friday night?"

"Are *you*?" Willie pulled the collar up on his coat.

"I asked first!" I said through chattering teeth.

"You two are impossible!" Lila exclaimed. It took us both by surprise.

"All right! Yes, I'm going." I answered.

"Good, because I already told my pa that you're riding with us!"

Chapter Twenty-one

I was on my best behavior all week. I didn't want to do anything that would jeopardize the all-night skating event. I did my chores without being asked, got my homework done, and got along with my siblings. Willie told me that Betty and Kathy were going and that Kathy's fiancé, Larry, would help chaperone and meet us there. Women from the area churches were bringing sandwiches and there would be music played on the organ by a man named Humphries. The idea was that kids could come and go any time. The only rule was that there would be no alcohol consumed at the rink and anyone found to have been drinking would be escorted home by one of the chaperones. We were told that there would be contests and games with prizes. It looked like it might be a fun night, in spite of the skating.

"Do you think they'll have a 'couples skate'?" Stella Johnson had asked after school.

Barb Bjornstad was right there to answer. "Of course not! It's a church thing and they don't let couples hold hands or anything!"

Stella shook her head, "I don't think that sounds like much fun."

"Why even worry about it? It's not like any of us has a boyfriend!" I blurted. But the girls both gave me glares.

"Did I say something wrong?"

At that moment, Willie walked by. "Pick you up around 7:30?"

"That sounds good," I replied.

"I'll see you then. I've gotta get right home and get my chores done," he said and jogged on ahead of us.

"What?" the girls said and rolled their eyes. "Right, Hildi ... none of *us* have *boyfriends*!"

We were all in a hurry to get home. I wanted to get my chores done and get cleaned up. Cedar Grove would be showing an outdoor movie for the kids who were too young to go to the skating event. It would be shown on the back of Anderson's General Store and would be a Laurel and Hardy film. Joe and Ben were excited and

Lila volunteered to pop popcorn for the family. Daddy had even said they could each have a bottle of soda pop while they watched.

After finishing my chores I ran to the house. It was 6:30 and I only had an hour to get ready. I dashed in the back door, kicked off my boots, hung up my coat, and whipped the scarf from my head.

"Hildi," Mom called from the dining room.

I was in a hurry and probably wore an impatient expression on my face when I went in to see what she needed.

"What is it?" I asked, entering the larger room.

She stood at the table where a pretty batch of blue fabric lay. But as I drew near, I saw that it wasn't just fabric, but a pretty cotton dress. She held it out to me with an expectant look in her eyes. This was not a store-bought dress, but my mother had sewn it by hand for me and kept it a secret until now.

I held it up and admired it. It was not overly fancy, but it didn't need to be. It had short sleeves, a sweetheart neckline, and a full skirt.

"I hope it fits. I had to do some guessing, but it should be pretty close. Go put it on, and we'll see if it's ok to wear tonight."

I dashed up to my bedroom and quickly changed into the dress. The fit was perfect and even without a full-length mirror I could tell that the shape was flattering.

I put on my dress shoes and went back down so Mom could see how it looked. She reached down and pulled on the hem and smoothed the full skirt. She had me turn as she looked closely at everything.

"Stop. I see something." She reached down and turned the hem over, revealing a forgotten straight pin. She pulled it out and pinned it to her blouse.

"What do you think?" She asked.

I was overwhelmed. Maybe I surprised myself because I never liked to wear dresses, but this was different ... I was different. With tears in my eyes, I hugged and thanked her.

"Say, you're running out of time. Go wash the cow-barn off your skin."

"I will! I'll take a bath! Thank you!" I called over my shoulder as I ran up the stairs.

I filled the tub with hot-water and lilac-scented bath salts, got in, and scrubbed. I put on a little makeup including lipstick and then I brushed my hair until it was slick and held back my long bangs with a pair of tortoise-shell barrettes. After making sure I was presentable both to the eye and to the nose, I dressed. It hadn't been a fluke; the dress still looked good and I felt pretty! I put on some of the rose-smelling perfume but not as much as I had put on the first day of school.

"Hildi!" Mom called from downstairs, "Willie is here."

I took one last look in the mirror and found a delicate white sweater to cover my arms from the chilly October air. Descending the stairs, I saw Willie standing in the dining room. He looked handsome in the jacket and tie. His hair was combed and his shoes shined. He walked up when I was on the last step and looked me over.

"You look real pretty, Hildi."

"So do you," I said, still standing on the bottom step.

We stared at each other a moment.

"You'd better get going." Mom stated.

I followed Willie out to the car where Chet waited in the driver's seat and Kathy and Betty sat in the back. Kathy opened the back door and got out.

"Here, slide in between Betty and me. Your legs are shorter."

Willie got in the front and we were off. The entire thirty-mile drive Kathy talked about her 'intended', Larry. Judging by the looks I observed from the other three, we couldn't get there fast enough.

Chapter Twenty-two

The skating rink had the appearance of a huge Quonset hut. It was a long building with an arched, corrugated-steel roof. The sides, however, were straight and built of concrete block. Light could enter from a large window in the front. On this night, the window was lit from the lights within. Cars were parked along the street for two blocks on both sides with more cars pulling up to the double doors and dropping off people of all shapes and sizes. Some were like us, young teens and older teens, excited for a long night of skating and fun, and others were members of the area churches, bringing in sandwiches and bars.

"Now remember, Hildi's papa will be here to pick you up at 6:00 tomorrow morning. Make sure you're ready before he gets here. Kathy, don't spend all your time with Larry. He's supposed to be helping to chaperone this crew."

"I know, Papa!" Kathy said irritably. I guessed it wasn't the first time she'd been reminded not to spend all her time with him.

"And you!" He pointed a finger at Willie, "You stay out of trouble!"

The boy held up a hand to signal that he'd gotten the message and we all went inside.

The sign at the counter read 'Skate Rental - 10 Cents'. The crowd around the counter was deep and full of the chatter of excited kids just like us. Kathy bypassed the skate rental counter and started looking for Larry, her fiancé. I recognized kids from our sister church in town as well as kids from our area who were in our 4H club. Virginia and George were there from our church, as well as my cousins, who had helped with our tobacco harvest. There had to be close to 200 kids at the rink. I wondered if there would be enough skates until I noticed many kids bringing in their own. Those must have been the town kids.

"Size?" asked a burly man behind the counter.

I hesitated while I thought.

"Shoe size?" He must have thought I didn't understand.   It was just that this was a new experience for me.

"Six." I said.   He disappeared and came back with a pair of white skates.   I put my dime on the counter and took the skates.

"Next."

Betty was next and stated her size without the hesitation I had.   Another person behind the counter waited on Willie and we were soon searching out a bench or a chair or someplace where we could sit down, remove our shoes, and put on the skates.   I was surprised that my skates were a bit tight and I felt awkward when I finally stood on them and tried to maneuver around.   So much for feeling pretty.

"There you are!"   I heard Kathy declare.

I looked near the tables of food to see her clutching a short, thin man.   He was wearing gold wire-rimmed spectacles and a serious expression with his tweed coat.   He gave her a quick kiss on the cheek and patted her hand.   His forehead was quite high and topped with hair that was light brown and slicked back.

"Kitty, you look beautiful tonight.   Are you going to help me supervise, or are you going to skate around and be one of the kids?"

Ignoring her father's admonition, she said, "I'm going to stay right by your side!"

The organ was already playing and a voice on a loudspeaker was announcing, "Welcome to the All-Night Skate here at the Ridgeview Roller Rink! Tonight's event is sponsored by the area churches. At 8:15, Reverend James Allison of Our Savior's Lutheran Church will be giving an opening prayer, so if you already have your skates on, that gives you ten minutes to try out the floor."

I felt like a cow trying to cross ice. A sturdy, short wall surrounded the wood floor of the rink itself and I clumsily skated to it and watched other kids gracefully glide around.

"Hi, Hildi!" called Barb Bjornstad as she passed on her way around. I waved and smiled as I held onto the wall for support.

Betty went by next and urged me to get on the floor, "Come on, Hildi!"

But I looked at the clock and it was getting close to time for the opening prayer. I pointed to the large round clock on the wall and turned back to watch more kids picking up skates at the counter. Just then, Andy Porter walked in carrying a large zippered bag. His gray wool jacket was open and I saw that he was dressed up as much as everyone else, he was even wearing a tie. He looked around the rink as though he was searching and then seemed to spot what he was looking for and waved. I followed his eyes to see

Willie, returning the wave with a nod. He made his way to Andy who found a chair and sat down. He unzipped the bag and drew out a pair of shiny black leather roller-skates.

"Good evening," announced a resonant voice over the loudspeaker. "On behalf of the area churches, welcome. Now let us have a moment of silence, and I will close with a word of prayer."

The rink quieted down and we bowed our heads. The prayer was given and the skating commenced. Andy took to the floor right away, gliding and turning and even skating backwards.

"Hi Hildi, what's the matter? Won't Willie skate with you?" Stella Johnson joined me at the wall where I watched.

"I'm no good at skating."

"Yeah, I know. Hey, is that Andy Porter out there?" Andy was at the far side of the rink.

I nodded.

"He is really good! And he cleans up nice, too!" She got on the floor and skated away towards him.

"Go get 'im, Stella," I said under my breath.

"Hildi!" I turned around to see Willie standing behind me. "Come on."

I shook my head, "No. Go on and have fun."

He held out his hand, "I am having fun. Come on."

I took his hand and he pulled me after him. But when I slipped and lost my balance before we ever got on the floor, he put his arm around my waist and said, "Loosen up. I've got you."

We stayed along the wall where the novice skaters skated.

"Relax. You're too stiff. You're thinking too much."

We skated around the rink one time. All the while, Willie encouraged me.

"See, you're doing all right."

"Because you won't let me fall!" I replied anxiously.

With that, he sped up and tightened his grip around my waist and we skated faster. We did several more revolutions before we had to get off the floor.

"Ladies and gentlemen, if you would clear the rink floor, we will set up our first contest."

We exited the floor and Willie dropped me off at a table where his sister Betty joined me.

"Now that looked like you were having fun, Hildi!" She handed me a glass of punch and sat next to me. "Don't lose that glass if you want any more punch!"

"Thanks! I guess it was fun, but I don't think I can skate by myself."

Betty smiled knowingly, "I'm going to tell you a secret."

I leaned across the table and looked into her brown eyes, "What is it?"

"Willie told me he's going to make sure you know how to skate before we leave tonight!"

I sat back in my chair. I didn't know if I should be happy for the attention or disgusted that I was becoming another 'project.' I instantly decided that I didn't care either way. I'd just enjoy the night.

"Go have a sandwich. There are lots of different kinds. You can check and see if Kathy and Larry are behaving!"

I got up and found it a bit easier to move on the skates. Larry and Kathy sat near the food table looking into each other's eyes. I looked over the sandwiches but there were also bars and cakes. Everything looked good and I hadn't had supper, so I took a sandwich and a lemon-poppy seed bar.

"Hildi, this is my fiancé Larry Slade."

Kathy made her introduction and Larry and I shook hands. I was taken aback at how soft and gentle his hands were. I was used to the grip of a farmer: a powerful grip with rough, calloused hands.

"Hello, Mr. Slade."

He grinned a big, crooked-toothed grin. It wasn't unpleasant but bright and honest. I liked him instantly. "So formal! You can call me 'Larry' ... unless you have me for a teacher next year. Then it is strictly 'Mr. Slade'!" He laughed easily.

"Are you going to watch the Limbo competition?" Kathy pointed to the line of kids gathering on the floor. Two of the ministers were there as well and they held what appeared to be a broomstick between them.

"What is it?" I'd never seen the 'limbo' before.

Larry answered but kept his eyes on the rink. "Skaters pass under a broomstick or a pole as they go around once. The men holding the broomstick or pole lower it each time everyone passes. Pretty soon, not everyone can get under the pole and they start to drop out. Eventually, that broomstick will be just a couple of feet off the floor and anyone who can't skate under it without touching the floor with their hands or any other part of their body is out."

Betty gestured for me to come back and pointed to the rink. Willie's suit jacket lay over the back of my chair, and I noticed that he was in a long line of teens already on the floor. Also in line were Andy Porter and Johnny Iverson. I joined Betty and ate my sandwich while we watched.

"This should be fun! The prize is a fly rod." She said excitedly.

The music started and the line began to move. No one was out on the first pass and the stick was lowered about six inches. Again, everyone passed under without any trouble. But as the game progressed, the men holding the pole became less generous, dropping it at least a foot or more until half the kids were out. Willie finally joined us at the table, but Andy and Johnny continued to skate until it was only those two. I did not know that Johnny was so flexible because he seemed so tall and awkward. But both he and Andy seemed to bend in two from the waist and glide under the broomstick. At this point, the broomstick was lowered incrementally and we watched intensely. With each successful pass, we cheered until the broomstick seemed to be just a couple feet from the floor. Andy was first and he spread his legs and leaned way back, but just as he had almost passed underneath, he lost his balance and fell on his backside. He got up and skated carelessly off to the side to see if Johnny would make it. Johnny used the same strategy but slowed way down, passing easily under the pole.

The rink erupted in a cheer and Andy skated out to shake Johnny's hand. Johnny was sent to the counter to pick up his prize.

"Come on." Willie again offered me his hand and we skated onto the floor, but this time, he didn't put his arm around my waist. We moved farther into the middle and skated together. The floor was becoming more crowded with some skaters passing us on the outside, but we kept going. Suddenly, Willie did something I didn't expect. He zoomed in front of me and turned to face me while skating backwards. He looked over his shoulder once and then back at me.

"Give me your other hand." I did. "Just look at me, don't look down and don't think about it."

For some reason it worked. We didn't get tangled up or fall down.

"Hildi, I've gotta do something tonight." He turned grave. "I need you to cover for me."

I met his attitude with my own, "Cover for you?"

"Listen, Andy's brothers are forcing him to stay in the Crenshaw house tonight. He has to be there by 11:00. I'm going, too."

I was beside myself, "Who says he's being *forced*? Did he tell you that? Are they holding a gun to his head?"

He rolled his eyes and they narrowed a bit as he answered me. "I just don't think he should be there alone. C'mon, Hildi. Help me out."

I was angry. I was selfish. I wanted this *night* and this *time* and everything had been going so well!

"Fine." I said hotly, let go of his hands, and skated off the floor. No one was at the table and I was alone for a while. I put my head in my hands and pouted. My feet hurt, so I unlaced the skates and took them off. When I looked up, I saw Andy helping himself to sandwiches and talking to some of the town kids. But soon Willie pulled him off to one side and I could see that the tone of the conversation was not for everyone to hear. Suddenly, I saw Andy wagging his head from side to side. Willie was gesturing as if to question his response.

"Look at my fly rod, Hildi!" Johnny sat down next to me, distracting me from the other two. He held out the fishing rod and I took it and looked it over, noting the polished wood and the stainless steel reel.

"It's a beauty! I can't wait to try it out ... even though I've never fished with a fly rod. I just have an old cane pole." He took back the rod and turned it over this way and that, looking at every detail.

"Congratulations, Johnny." Willie skated up behind us, but I didn't look at him.

"I bet Larry and Kathy will watch that for you if you want to get back in the rink."

"Do you think they would? That would be great. Otherwise, I'll end up carrying this thing around all night!"

Willie nodded and Johnny skated off towards the food.

Willie sat next to me, "Hildi, will you listen to me?"

I looked at him but I didn't change my expression.

"I told Andy I'd go with him, but he said that would just make things worse. I guess his brothers don't think he can last the night, so they're going to lock him in. There's a padlock on the door."

That sounded like a recipe for danger. If anything was to happen, how would he get out? How could he get help?

I looked at the clock. It didn't seem like we'd been there very long, but it was already 10:00. I had an idea.

"He shouldn't be alone," I admitted. "Let's follow him, both of us. We can go and come back and just keep checking on him. What do you think?"

"Hildi ..."

"Listen to me before you tell me 'no.' Do you think no one is going to notice if you disappear? Do you think Betty's not going to notice? You need to tell her about this so she knows and doesn't panic. You have to have a reason to leave!"

***

Andy ducked out at 10:15. I don't know what Willie told Betty, but he assured me that she would not worry. We decided to give Andy a few minutes before following him. The Crenshaw house was on the other side of town and it would take at least half an hour to get there. I put on my shoes and Willie changed out of his skates. We ate more sandwiches and cake and watched other people skate. He was reaching for his suit coat when a voice came over the loudspeaker.

"Boys and girls, may I have your attention, please? The next skate will be a 'couples' skate. If you are here with a special someone, this next skate is for you."

The lights began to go down and Willie looked across the table at me, "Put your skates back on."

"What?"

He was already untying his shoes and getting his skates around, "Put your skates back on and hurry it up."

The music started, the lights grew dim, and couples began to enter the rink. Willie, just like before, offered me his hand, and we skated onto the floor. My heart raced!

"Here," he said.

He put his left arm around my waist, making me aware of how warm he was next to me. With his left hand, he held my right, and with his right hand, he held my left so that my arms were crossed in front of me and we were pulled close together. The smell of Ivory soap and a little Bay Rum aftershave was in the air.

"You smell nice," I said.

He looked pleased, "My pa's aftershave ... it was his idea."

"I like it."

After that, we really didn't say any more. We skated easily, in time to the music. There was no need to show off or to rush. While some of the couples did fancy spins, changing places and looking like ballroom dancers, we skated together in perfect unison. No one else in the room existed, just Willie and me. Every so often we would glance at each other and smile.

We were on the far end of the rink when the song ended and the lights slowly came up. It was a little darker down there, but there was a light in Willie's eyes.

"I'm glad we stayed a little longer." He said quietly, still holding my hands.

"Me, too." I meant it.

Chapter Twenty-three

It was chilly outside and, with Ridgeview being on the ridge, the wind was blowing. I pulled the sweater tighter around my shoulders and clipped along beside Willie. Our last skate put us behind Andy by more than fifteen minutes.

The streets were lined with old houses. Many of them were big Victorian homes with castle-like towers. Some stood three stories high and many were in poor condition. These homes were left over from lumber barons and railroad tycoons who were prominent in the area fifty to seventy years earlier. Most of these homes were dark, but a few were occupied. Some had wrought iron fences surrounding the property. Some had hedges instead, but all sat on large dark lots. The depression had brought many of the properties to their current dilapidated condition. The darkness around them was overwhelming. But the bright harvest moon gave off enough light to illuminate the street, but eerie, ominous shadows seemed to lurk everywhere.

We walked for a long time and I grew colder by the minute until my fingers and toes grew numb. Finally, we came to the far end of town and to an area that seemed isolated.

"There it is, right up there. Do you see it?" Willie stopped and pointed.

"No," I answered, my chattering teeth giving me away.

I was so cold but I wasn't about to turn back or complain. I rubbed my arms and tried to keep my teeth from chattering as I looked down the street. But what caught my attention was the huge cemetery on the opposite side of the street. It was surrounded with a wrought iron fence, like some of the old mansions. At the entrance was a tall hinged gate and above it, in large letters the name 'Shady Oaks Cemetery'. There weren't any locks or chains on the gate.

I thought I saw something or someone looking out from behind the tombstones. I strained to see, but the wind was moving the trees. The leaves that fell blew around us, making it impossible to tell if it was anything to be concerned about or just my wild imagination playing tricks on me. Willie's voice shook me. I glanced at him and when I looked back, whatever I had seen had vanished.

"Hildi, you're freezing! Maybe you should go back."

I shook my head fiercely, "I'm going with you!"

"All right, then, take my jacket." He quickly took off his suit coat and put it around my shoulders. It was warm and I instantly began to feel better.

He stuck his hands deep into his pockets and tried to pretend that he wasn't feeling the nip in the air.

We started walking again. We passed the cemetery and then I saw the Crenshaw house. I'd seen the Crenshaw house once or twice before but that was from inside a car or truck. It looked different from ground level. It was bigger. This house was massive. Built of quarried yellow limestone, it dwarfed the other houses we'd passed. But like many of the other houses, it sat on a dark lot. Its wrought iron gate and surrounding fence were in a sad state with sections missing and a tangle of old ivy covered most of it. Huge windows yawned down at onlookers while the oaken front door barred intruders. The side of the house that faced the street had a small balcony on the second floor.

At once I knew that this was where August Crenshaw had stood as he defied those who wanted to bring him to justice. I again felt a chill, but it wasn't from the cold air. It ran up and down my spine as I fought the tinge of fear I felt. I'd almost forgotten that this was the anniversary of August Crenshaw's suicide.

Willie pushed a small latch up and the gate swung open with a noisy squeak. We passed through it and he turned back to make sure the gate latched again.

"Hey, I can see Andy!" I noticed a figure in the upstairs window which led to the balcony. I waved, but he didn't wave back. A strange and heavy feeling of dread settled upon me.

"Where do you see him?" Willie asked.

I pointed to the balcony window, but he was gone.

"He's not there now." Willie sounded frustrated, "He's probably gonna tell us to get lost!"

I was puzzled, "Get lost?"

Willie's teeth were chattering now, "He told me that he has to do this alone or his brothers will make his life miserable. He can't keep living like this, Hildi! He's a bully because it's all he knows! He has to know there's another way."

The long path to the house had once been paved with cobblestone but was now overgrown with moss and worn down. When we reached the front door we saw a padlock that was meant to keep trespassers out. Andy's dad had placed the lock on the door to protect the house and any equipment he had stored for the project.

Willie tapped tentatively on the door. There was no response. He rapped a bit louder. Again, there was no response. He tried again, but this time he pounded hard and the sound seemed to carry in the dark.

A figure appeared in the window near the front door. It was Andy.

"What are you doing here?" The muffled question came through the window.

"We wanted to check on you to see if you're all right. Do you need anything?" Willie's voice shook with the chill.

"What?"

Willie cleared his throat and prepared to yell louder but Andy motioned for him to stop. He reached up and moved something on the window, then pushed it up until it opened.

"Hey!" Andy leaned out of the large window. It was about five feet off the ground. "What are you doing here? I told you ... I have to do this alone!"

Willie went to the window. I could see the gooseflesh under his white cotton dress shirt. "I know ... and I told Hildi, so it's not any kind of a secret."

Andy looked at me ruefully, then back at Willie.

"Look, you need to go back. If Gabe and Sam come ..."

"If Gabe and Sam come where will we hide? Let us keep you company for a while. I bet there are more hiding places in there than out here. Besides, I'm freezing my ears off!"

Andy stuck his head further out the window and looked towards the street and then back to Willie. "I can't let you in the door, you know. You'd have to come in this window and I don't think she can do it."

"I've seen her climb. She'll make it."

He was thoughtful a moment. "Ok. I guess you can come in for a little while, but you've got to climb up here and through the window and I still don't think she can do it in that dress."

To that I replied, "Watch me!"

Willie looked my way and then zoned in on my feet, "Take off your shoes."

My expression said, 'huh?'

Willie explained, "I'll get down and you can use my back for a step. Will you at least give her a hand if she asks for it?"

"Yeah, just hurry up."

I took off my shoes and was struck at how cold the ground was beneath my feet. Willie got down on all fours and made himself as sturdy as he could. I took hold of the wall beneath the window. The limestone was rough and that made it easy to grip. I stepped up onto Willie's back and he lifted himself up as much as he could. Climbing in this window would be easy compared to scaling the big bluffs around our farms. The only thing I didn't like was climbing in wearing a dress.

"Give me your hand." I directed.

He furrowed his brow. I suppose he didn't expect me to be so eager to climb in a window, but he reached down and grasped my hand. He pulled and I placed a foot against the limestone blocks. If I'd been dressed right, I could have scaled that wall without any help, but in a dress it was another matter. Andy pulled and soon I was climbing over the window sill.

My shoes suddenly came flying through the window and landed on the floor with a clatter. I retrieved them quickly and put them on. As soon as I did, Willie was climbing through the window and into the entryway.

Andy shook his head, "I don't get it? What is it with you? I told you I'd be all right, didn't I?"

Willie rubbed his arms and blew into his hands. Unlike either of us, Andy wore a wool jacket. It was warmer inside than out. A tall candle stood in a bottle on the floor and gave out the only light. It flickered and the shadows it cast seemed to dance on the floor and walls. I had an uneasy feeling about being here. And it wasn't because of Andy.

"What were you doing upstairs?" I asked curiously.

Suddenly, there was a loud noise as if a shelf of pans had collapsed. We all jumped.

"Where did that come from?" Willie's eyes were wide.

"I don't know!" exclaimed Andy. But he reached down and picked up the candle and began to walk in the direction from where the sound had come. We stayed where we were.

"Well?" he turned suddenly, "Are you coming or not?"

We followed quickly. It was obvious that the place had been under some kind of renovation but that the work had been stopped in the middle of the job. Piles of broken plaster and lathe lay in each room. Wires hung between some of the studs and from the ceiling, as well.

Each room we entered and left showed no signs of anyone or anything being in them recently. Most unsettling was the fact that no room had anything metallic which had fallen and made the type of impact we had just heard. We searched every room on the main floor and finally entered the last room, the 'great room'.

Even though the candle gave off some light, the greatest illumination came from the full moon that passed through the tall, dusty old windows. In that moonlight I could see a magnificent room. The remnants of a grand staircase rose to a balcony and second floor while the ceiling of the room stretched beyond the second floor, making it a good sixteen feet in height. The railing along the staircase had been removed and carefully laid out in sections on the floor below. The remaining railing was along the second floor hallway which overlooked the great room and led to other rooms above. Perhaps there had been parties and dances, and those who had lived here had made spectacular entrances down those stairs. I could only imagine the splendor of those days.

I left my imagination on the stairway and turned back to reality. The walls had been stripped of their lathe and plaster, leaving only the two-by-four studs. Now it was a skeleton of what had been.

"What do you suppose that was?" Willie inquired, "What about upstairs? Could it have been a rat knocking something over?"

Andy shook his head and looked about, "Maybe. I don't know."

"Shouldn't we keep checking?" I asked.

Andy didn't move but seemed to be staring at something. Willie and I looked at each other.

"Andy?" he said.

At last Andy shook his head, "It's gotta be Sam or Gabe! I bet they set a bunch of stuff up here to try to scare me all night!"

I could believe that.

"Then let's find everything first!" exclaimed Willie. "Then the joke will be on them and you'll have the last laugh."

Finally, Andy smiled at Willie. It was a genuine smile, not sarcastic because he'd gotten even or done some dirty trick. It improved his looks, at least to me.

"All right! Let's go, but be careful. Some of the floorboards are weak or have dry rot. We were going to rip up the floors and do those repairs when Dobkins shut everything down. And if you're still here when my brothers show up, you've got to stay out of sight!"

"Agreed," I replied.

We began with the first floor. All in all, when the mansion was first built, it contained twenty-one large rooms. But when the mansion served as an apartment house, those rooms had been divided. The demolition phase of Porter's work had been to tear out walls and re-establish those rooms to their original spaciousness. Some rooms were like the great room. All lathe and plaster had been removed just leaving the bare studs, while other rooms had been left untouched.

We passed through a hallway behind the great room and near a closed door. Some metal scaffolding crossed the width of the hallway.

"Watch those floorboards! If you step on them, you'll go right through," Andy pointed directly in front of me. Although I followed him and Willie, I hadn't noticed that they had sidestepped the area.

I quickly stepped around the floorboards but bumped the scaffolding.

"And watch that scaffolding!"

Willie grabbed me by the arm and pulled me next to him. Just as he did, a large brick dropped right where I had been standing.

"That wall separates the kitchen from the rest of the house. It's brick and we were taking it down. You have to start with the bricks on top first. That top plank is filled with bricks. You don't want any of them to land on your head!"

We searched each room but turned up nothing. Once, we were startled by a very large rat, but other than that, there was nothing. We went back to the great room and stood beneath the balcony, near the stairway.

"Let's try upstairs. Watch the steps. The railing is gone and ..."

We all felt a sudden wisp of cool air. The candle flickered and went out.

"You're not funny, Cooper! I don't have another match!"

"I didn't do anything."

We all searched the shadows, looking for the source of the breeze when we all saw something that made our blood run cold. There, on the wall in front of us was the shadow of a noose!

"Where's that coming from?" cried Andy.

Willie turned to the upper windows and hunted, "It's gotta be from a window or something ..."

And as quickly as it had been there, it vanished.

I could hear the trembling in Andy's breathing. "We have to get out of here!"

Just then, there was a clicking in the lock of the front door, the sound carrying through the hollow rooms to where we stood. This was accompanied by giggles.

"It's your brothers," Willie whispered.

Andy pulled himself together, "Go back to the kitchen and wait."

We went back to a room we had been in only moments earlier. It was dark and no light from the moon seemed to pass through the bank of windows that overlooked the old carriage and servant houses. This was where the back door was located. Willie tried the handle. It turned but wouldn't open. It had been padlocked, too.

"Do you really think Andy's brothers are doing this?" I whispered.

Willie didn't answer right away. He gazed out the window intently.

"Are you sure you saw Andy in the window upstairs?"

"I saw someone. Who else would it be?"

"I don't know. But ... maybe we're being set up, Hildi. Maybe Andy and his brothers are playing us for a couple of rubes."

That gave me little comfort, except for one possibility. "Willie, what if they're not. What if what they say is true and this place is haunted?"

"Greater is He that is in me ..." he answered with assurance.

"What is that?" I asked.

"Hildi, come on! Last year it was you who kept pointing me in the right direction! I don't believe in ghosts. And if this house has anything, it might be possessed by demons, but even if that is the case, God is greater! We have nothing to fear."

There was a sound and we both looked towards the door to see the flicker of the candle as Andy returned. He held the candle, once again lit, in one hand and a book of matches in the other.

"They gave me some matches in case the candle goes out again. Sam told me to be handy next time they showed up so they don't have to hunt for me."

Willie looked at him hard, "So ... you're ok?"

"There's nothin' wrong with me!" he growled. "We'll go upstairs."

We went back to the great room and followed Andy as he began to ascend the staircase. Some of the steps were broken and each one creaked as pressure was put upon it. We were about half way up when Andy stopped and pointed to the center of the great room.

"It was right there, in that area, where we were set up to work on the wiring for the chandelier and where Eldon Grimm, he worked for my dad, fell and broke his leg."

I tried to imagine how the scaffolding had looked as Andy went on in his explanation. The fall had to be a good fifteen foot drop onto the floor below.

We continued to the top of the steps and again, Andy warned us to be careful, especially of the remaining railing.

"Fifty years ago it might have been strong enough to hold a man's full weight. But if August Crenshaw tried to hang himself from it today, he'd be more likely to get a broken neck from the fall when it gives way!"

We chuckled and followed him into the first room. This room was different from the rooms on the first floor. The walls were still intact and the linoleum was still on the floor. Most of the rooms were in a similar state and I found that it was slightly warmer on this second floor than it was on the first. I noticed Willie continuing to blow on his hands and I tried to return his jacket. But he refused it. I felt guilty for being warm but even more so for not thinking to wear a fall coat to the skating rink.

Once again, we found nothing.

"This is where Crenshaw was when they came after him." Andy was doing a great job as a tour guide.

We entered the room with the walk-out window and balcony. Willie took a seat on the cast iron radiator. You could easily see the street from here as well as the front door. I noted that this was the smallest of the second story rooms. It surprised me. I had envisioned a much larger room, nearer the hallway and staircase. I'd never seen pictures of the interior of the mansion but had relied on my own imagination.

"He held them off for hours from here. He was armed with a forty-four revolver. And then, after all that, he hangs himself!"

He looked at Willie, "Does that make any sense to you?"

Willie shrugged, "He was guilty and he didn't have any hope. If the town caught him, they probably would have lynched him. If he went to trial, he probably would have gotten life in prison ... *if he made it to prison alive*. He was paying for his crimes, his sins."

"What's 'sin' got to do with it?" Andy leaned against the window and stared down at the lawn. "My mom is like you ... religious. She tries to teach us one way and Pop turns around and teaches us another. She never wins."

"What do you think would happen if she did? What if you stopped trying to get even for every wrong you think is done to you?"

Andy snorted, "Then I'd be weak! I'd be like you ... "

He stopped short, realizing what he'd just said. A couple of weeks earlier he wouldn't have stopped, but now he did.

"I'm ... sorry."

Willie stood up, "No. I *am* weak. We're all weak. We all do stupid things. We all sin. There is no perfect man on this earth today and there never will be. There was only one and He paid for our sins. August Crenshaw didn't know Him so he had to pay for his own sins ..."

Andy shook his head, "No, you're not gonna get all religious on me, Cooper!"

"All right. I won't say anything else. But when you're ready to hear it, I'll tell you everything you need to know."

"That'll be a long time coming."

Chapter Twenty-four

Thus far, our investigations had turned up nothing. We hadn't found any access points into the house from the back that weren't locked with a padlock and it appeared that the only working window was the one we had come through. Oh, the others might work with a crowbar and some elbow grease, but they hadn't been opened that night. Andy was becoming more amiable as time passed. But in the back of my mind, I wondered if anyone would be missing us at the rink.

"They had dances up there," Andy said as we approached a smaller open stairway with a railing on one side.

"On the third floor?" I blurted, "That's hard to believe."

Although the stairway was smaller, it was wide enough to allow two to ascend side by side. These steps seemed in better condition than the others. There was a short landing in front of a closed door. Willie turned the handle, but the door was swollen and wouldn't budge. He had taken the candle from Andy and now turned to me.

"Can you hold this?"

Willie handed me the candle, turned back to the door, and hit it hard with his shoulder. The door stood firm and he tried again with no obvious result. Willie rubbed his shoulder.

"Maybe you should give it a shot." He gestured towards the door and Andy stepped up.

He also tried shoving it open using his shoulder, but it didn't yield on the first try. Again he hit it but this time it moved a little.

"I gotta tell you, we haven't done anything up here. This is really stuck! I can see how you hurt your shoulder, Cooper."

He hit it a third time and it burst open. I noticed Willie still rubbing his shoulder but not in the place he'd used against the door. He was rubbing the place where he'd been wounded just seven months earlier. I found it odd that it should bother him now. Andy took the candle, entered the room, and we followed.

Even in the flickering light of the candle this room was impressive. The ceiling rose to a peak with exposed hand-hewn beams. Its slope followed the contour of the roof, making the room long but a bit narrow at the slope. A few wooden chairs stood along the wall. I imagined a row of chairs on either side of the room where dancers waited to be asked to dance or maybe they watched while others danced. A chimney rose on the far end of the wall and in front of it was a rusty cast iron stove. The room appeared untouched, having never been turned into apartments.

There were other items in the room, old paintings, a broken mirror and a wooden box that appeared to contain pictures. Andy set the candle on the stove where it illuminated most of the room. I picked up the pictures. Willie had stopped rubbing his shoulder, but rolled it every so often. Andy watched him intently, but Willie didn't notice. He was lifting one of the paintings and holding it up to catch the dancing light. It was a portrait that was none too flattering of its female subject.

"I can see why this is up here," he made a disgusted face and leaned the picture back against the wall.

"Hey, Cooper ... Will, when you were at my house ... my mom said she saw ..."

'Andy!'

"You hear that?" Andy whispered.

"Andy!"

The voice was much clearer and I recognized it! The look on Andy's face concerned me.

"You can't be here!" he rasped. "They can't know you're with me! Stay up here!"

He grabbed the candle and disappeared out the door. We heard his feet on the stairs and his voice carried back up to us. "Whadya want? It hasn't been an hour yet!"

"What are you doing up there?"

"I'm just checkin' things out, you know, lookin' the place over, see?"

The voices began to fade, "We were gonna bring you a bottle but ..."

The room had a small, round window near the peak of the roof with the outline of a five-pointed star inside. A tiny stream of moonlight passed through that window and touched the floor in front of me. It wasn't much. It should have been brighter, but maybe a cloud was covering the moon. I could barely make out the outline of the stove, but Willie's white shirt showed up well.

"What are we doing?" I asked.

"Meeting a need." He breathed, "Can you see where I am 'cause I can't see you at all?"

I was still wearing his jacket and it covered up my white sweater.

"I can see where you are. Do you want your jacket back?" I asked, again.

"No. Come here."

I crossed to where he stood and wondered what he wanted.

"I can kind of see you now." He said.

He reached out and touched my shoulders, traced them down to my elbows, and finally touched my hands. He took them firmly, "I think we should pray. Something here isn't right and maybe it's just me but ..."

"No," I cut in, "I feel it, too. Like a weight. You start this time."

Willie and I bowed our heads in the dark, "Father in Heaven, thank you. Thank you for hearing us and giving us hope. Lord, we ask for You to help us tonight with whatever is happening, or going to happen. Lord, we ask You to open Andy's eyes, touch his heart and help him to know that he needs Jesus ..."

"Dear God," I prayed, "You know our hearts, our minds and You know everything. Lord, please protect all of us tonight. Send Your angels to keep watch. And help me to put aside my feelings of doubt about Andy, to give him a chance and love him like Jesus would ... and does, in Jesus' name, amen."

When we prayed together, we always held hands and let go on 'amen', but tonight he held mine a little longer.

"You smell nice tonight, too." He added.

Still curious about another matter, I asked, "What did you tell Betty before we left?"

Right at that moment, Andy returned and the candle light revealed us holding hands. We quickly let go and stepped away from each other.

"Now I know why you're here!" cried Andy, "You wanted some place to be alone!"

"No!"

"No!"

Our denials tumbled over each other's and Andy laughed about it. He put the candle back on the stove and I picked up the pictures I'd been looking at. They were stiff and yellowed. The faces ranged from mild to stern and even aloof. Most of the pictures were formal portraits, a woman sitting and a man standing with his hand on her shoulder, or the reverse. But some were larger in size with big groups of people, perhaps a family reunion or some kind of social gathering that had been photographed for posterity. While I studied the pictures, I listened to Willie and Andy.

"They said they'd come back every hour to make sure I haven't hung myself. But they came back early. I don't have a watch, but I know they're early."

"Your brothers are some jokers."

"'Jerks' is more like it."

"And you want to be just like them ..." Again, Willie reached for his shoulder and I could barely make out his face when he grimaced.

"No, I don't ... I don't know. They're tough and people respect them."

"They're mean and people are afraid of them. That's no way to get respect."

I had been thumbing through the pictures with interest when I reached to the bottom of the box and discovered an old book and I pulled it out. It was not large. The cover was once black cloth but now faded to a dark gray. I couldn't make out the writing, so I went to the candle on the stove and tilted the book. As I did, the candle flickered and went out. But before it did, I clearly saw a pentagram embossed on the cover of the book.

"Hildi!" Andy cried, "What did you do?"

"I didn't do anything! It just went out when I tried to look at this book."

"Just a minute." Almost instantly there was a scratch and a spark as Andy struck a match. He crossed the room and re-lit the candle.

I lifted the book and again turned it towards the light and again the candle flickered and went out, but this time, Andy could see that I had done nothing to extinguish the flame. The moonlight that passed through the window seemed to grow brighter. But when it touched the floor I noticed that the outline from the window formed a pentagram just like the one on the book.

Andy struck another match and lit it a third time. This time I backed away from the candle and turned the book. There was writing embossed around the pentagram, *'Spiritualism, Sorcery, and Spells'*. I opened the cover to read the inscription written inside: *Property of August J. Crenshaw.*

"Cooper, what's the matter with you?"

In the yellow, flickering light, I saw Willie sitting on one of the wooden chairs along the wall, his face was pale.

"I don't know ... " His hand was below his shoulder, the same place where his wound had been, just an inch or so below his collar bone.

I dropped the book back into its box and rushed to him.

Andy retrieved the candle.

I knelt beside the chair and placed my hand on his. I was shocked at how hot it was, almost burning! When I tried to look, he held it there firmly.

"Let me see it," I demanded.

"Cooper ... I started to say something before ... about that shoulder ..." The tone of Andy's voice was rising. "When you were at my house and my mom was taping up your ribs, she said she saw a scar ..."

"Not now, Andy!" I yelled.

Willie groaned as I tugged his hand away, revealing a spreading bloody stain on his shirt! Andy swore when he saw it.

This was impossible! There was no hole. That wound had healed months ago. But the pain he felt was real and the panic rising in me was real. I undid the knot in Willie's tie and tried to unbutton the buttons of his shirt, but my fingers were numb and didn't want to work. It was as though I had to will them to move. All the while, Willie was passing into delirium, and Andy was becoming hysterical. I worked frantically.

"What is that?" Andy cried, but I ignored him.

"Help me get him on the floor!" I ordered.

We guided Willie off the chair and onto the plank floor. I was about to open his shirt in order to find out where the blood was coming from when suddenly, the open door slammed shut and the candle went out. The little stream of moonlight that had made it possible for us to see in the dark was gone, covered by clouds or some unseen force. Even the pentagram had vanished. In the darkness and silence was the sound of our frenzied breathing. Neither of us moved. A cold breeze passed through the room, yet there was no door or window open. My hand was on Willie's chest. He was sweating but trembling at the same time, and his breathing was rapid. I could feel his heart racing. What was all this?

"Dear God in Heaven, please, help us!" I called out loud.

Instantly, something changed. Whatever had covered the moonlight, be it clouds or some demonic veil, lifted and it streamed in again. Willie breathed a deep, long sigh. There was a change in his heartbeat and I felt his chest rise and fall as his breathing slowed. In the darkness I felt a presence, a hand placed over mine and another on my shoulder. And, finally ... peace. In that moment, the words *I am here, don't be afraid* calmed my being.

Finally, I dared to speak, "Light the candle, Andy."

Again, the scratch, a whiff of sulfur and the yellow, flickering glow of the candle. Willie's eyes were closed and he breathed easier now. I looked down in order to find the source of blood that had spread over his shirt. But when I did, it was gone! The shirt was white again! I pulled it wide open, revealing the scar, still pink, the wound healed as it had been for months.

Andy's knees hit the floor with a thud. He grabbed Willie's shirt and searched it. He pulled it and twisted it. "I know what I saw! Where did it go? Where is it?"

He looked at me, "You saw it!"

I nodded.

"Well, where is it? Where's the blood?"

Willie's eyes moved beneath the lids and he stirred, "God is greater ..."

"What did he say?" Andy drew closer.

Willie opened his eyes and I pulled him up next to me. He looked at me weakly. Whatever had just happened seemed to have zapped his strength.

"God is greater." I repeated. "I think we've just been attacked by something evil, but God is greater. He stopped whatever was happening, not us."

"Hildi?" Willie murmured, and shivered in the chill of the attic room.

"What?"

"I'll take my jacket back now."

Chapter Twenty-five

We left the third floor. Willie was drained but able to walk without help. The fact was that all of us were drained from our experience in the attic. Yet, I was thankful for having experienced God's love and protection and I breathed a prayer of thanksgiving.   On the other hand, Andy was terrified. I knew this was getting harder for him. His brothers had challenged him to stay all night, but I could tell he was ready to leave. Doing that, though, would bring on their wrath, maybe even his father's taunts.

"Are you still going to stay?" I asked.

He looked miserable. "I have to! I can't go anywhere."

"You could go back to the skating rink with us."

We stopped at the top of the grand staircase.

"Can we sit a minute," Willie asked and swayed a little, "I feel kind of dizzy and I don't want to roll down these stairs."

Andy led us back to the room with the window balcony where we had been earlier. Willie leaned against the wall and slid to the floor. Andy joined him on one side and I was on the other.

"What happened to you, Cooper? That scar, I mean. And what is that ... or was that ..."

Exhausted from the encounter in the attic, Willie kept his eyes shut as he began to explain our adventure last spring. As I listened, I leaned over and buttoned up his shirt.

"I got that scar from a man named Emmit Romney. He was a bank robber who got out of prison last March. Twenty years ago, he hid a box of gold coins in a cave between our farm and Hildi's. And it was close to that cave when he got caught by the sheriff, Hildi's grandpa, Albert Barnum. As soon as Romney got out of prison, he headed right for that gold, but first, he showed up at Barnum's sugar bush. As far as we know, we think he was probably gonna kill her grandpa that night. But her grandpa wasn't there. It was just the two of us. In the dark, he mistook me for Hildi's grandpa and shot me. Then, he held us hostage while he hunted for the cave and the gold. But things didn't work out the way he'd planned it. I'd already found the gold and moved it to a different cave 'til I could figure out what to do with it." His voice grew weaker and weaker until he dozed off. His head dropped onto my shoulder.

I continued the story. I filled in the gaps until Andy heard it all, including Romney's escape from jail, his kidnapping of Willie, our encounter at the old grist mill, and how Lila saved our lives.

"Romney wanted revenge. He didn't just want the money, he wanted to get even. But you're never even. When he first got out of prison, he could have told the FBI where the money was hidden. When he escaped from jail, he could have gone to Canada and started over. But he wanted to settle the score. There was this fellow named Charlie Kiley who tried to get him to turn himself in, to accept Jesus, and find forgiveness. But, Romney refused to listen. He was dead in less than an hour. In a way, Willie's been trying to show you what Charlie tried to tell Romney. All that time spent trying to get even is wasted. You might try to get even with men, but you're never even with God."

"Why didn't anybody tell me what happened to him, to you? Why didn't *he* tell me?" He asked intensely, referring to Willie.

My own eyes had grown weary; maybe the *house* was draining me, too.

"I suppose everybody at school heard about it, and talked about it so much over the summer that it just wore itself out." I answered, "Willie's just a normal kid. He doesn't want people to like him or treat him better because they think he's a hero."

"I would have." He said quietly.

"He knows that. That's why he didn't tell you."

Willie mumbled something incoherent but continued to doze and the sound of his deep, even breaths were the only thing we heard inside. Outside, the wind howled, and in the distance, the bell on the clock-tower of the county courthouse chimed one. I listened to the deep, resonant peel. It was clear over on the other side of town, but it carried on the wind.

"You *can* be nice," I said, breaking the silence. Andy looked at me so I continued. "And when you're like this, like tonight, I don't mind being around you. You should try being nice more often."

He didn't say anything, but I noticed a smile that he tried to hide by looking away.

"By-the-way, what were you doing up here before we came?" I ventured.

Andy looked confused, "What are you talking about?"

I clarified, "When we came in the gate, I looked up here at this window and saw you. I waved at you but you didn't wave back."

He leaned forward and looked at me, "I wasn't up here before you came."

"Ha, ha! I say something nice to you and now you have to joke with me."

"No. I'm not joking. I wasn't up here. My brothers had just left before you got here. They started out by only giving me one match and told me to make it work on that candle or I'd be sitting alone in the dark. In this drafty old house, I was trying to make sure the candle lit."

I thought back to the figure in the window. Andy was wearing a gray wool jacket. Whoever I had seen in the window appeared to be dressed in black. Who had I seen? What had I seen? Could it have been the *ghost* of August Crenshaw, or my over-active imagination?

Willie took a deep breath and held it a moment as he woke up and stretched. He opened his mouth, yawned noisily, and sat up, rubbing his eyes.

There was a loud creak and the sound of a door being shut.

"That must be my brothers. You stay here, out of sight. If I decide to call it quits and go back to the rink, I don't want them to think you had anything to do with it."

He got up and took the candle with him.

I turned to look at Willie. He fiddled with his tie, attempted to re-tie the knot, but quickly gave up. But he looked refreshed, despite being all thumbs with the tie.

"Do you feel alright? I mean, do you even know what happened up there?"

"I felt hot, like I was on fire, and my shoulder ... it hurt like everything, like something was boring into it ..." he remembered.

I nodded, "We saw blood, Willie, all over your shirt. It was as if you'd been shot again. And when I touched your hand it felt like you were burning up. I think you passed out."

"I'm fine, Hildi. You don't need to worry about me."

"It scared me, Willie. What was happening to you, I mean. But the strangest ... no, the most wonderful thing happened. It stopped when I called out to the Lord." I said.

We were both thoughtful a moment until I remembered what seemed to have started the entire ordeal on the third floor.

"That book I was looking at, it was about sorcery. That's witchcraft, isn't it?"

"Yeah," he confirmed.

"It belonged to August Crenshaw. His name was on the inside. Do you think he was doing things like that, like trying to contact the dead or trying to cast spells?"

Willie pulled his knees up to his chest and hugged them, "My grandma once told me that there was a handful of young men in town that called themselves the 'Enlightened Young Gentlemen's Club'. They had money, came from rich families. They did a lot of traveling to other countries. They studied on a lot of other religions, especially spiritualism and calling on the dead. She said that they held things called séances, talked to fortune tellers and such. She said something like they got more and more involved in the occult. And all of them met tragic ends. Crenshaw was the first. The second one fell overboard on a ship that was headed for the West Indies and he drowned. A third slipped on the ice and hit his head so hard it killed him. The fourth was poisoned by his wife, and the last one was knifed in an alley here in town."

"Whatever happened upstairs ... whatever is happening in this house isn't human, Willie. I think you were right when you said this house could be possessed by demons. What happened to you, that was real. I know what we saw. And when I called on him, the Lord rescued us."

"I'll sure be glad to get home."

I remembered that I had asked him a question earlier that never got answered. "What did you tell Betty?"

He raised his eyebrows and smiled, "Oh, something so she wouldn't worry about us but know that we're together."

"And what exactly was that?" I pressed, but he wouldn't say.

He stood up and again tried to re-shape the knot.

"Did you take this out? It was just perfect, so I could get it on and off without having to re-tie it."

I got up and stood in front of him. "Who tied it for you last time?"

He looped one end over the other, wrapped it around itself, and ended up with a mess.

"Kathy. And she told me it was the last time she was tying my tie for me."

I took the ends out of his hands, "Every man should learn how to tie his own tie. I've got two little brothers and they can both tie their own ties. You aren't always going to have someone like a sister around to tie your tie for you, so it's very important that you learn how to do this on your own. There. All done."

I slid the knot up to his throat tightly.

"That's called a half Windsor. I can tie a full Windsor, too. I'll show you some time."

He pursed his lips, reached up, and loosened it as it had been before. He looked around and wrinkled his nose.

"Do you smell something? Is that smoke?"

"And kerosene!" I added. "Andy's been gone too long."

An unmistakable glow illuminated the great room and smoke wafted up from below.

"The house is on fire!" I exclaimed.

Chapter Twenty-six

We raced down the steps to the front door which was still shut. Willie tried it, but it wouldn't budge. The window was shut, too. Willie opened it but as he did, we heard a voice.

"Help! Help me!"

"That came from the kitchen!"

Willie left the window open and turned towards the sound. We couldn't go back through the great room because it had been engulfed by the blaze. So we took an adjacent hallway. When we did, I saw an empty gallon can of kerosene on its side and the candle Andy had carried, now broken, on the floor.

We circled around through what had once been a formal dining room, passed a second, smaller room, to the back hallway where the kitchen and back door were located. I was careful to sidestep the rotted floorboards and avoided the scaffolding with the bricks on the top plank.

A beam of light shined through the open door.

"Please, Mister," Andy's voice pleaded, "You don't have to do this! You don't have to kill me!"

"I'm sorry, boy. Nobody was supposed to be here. But I can't leave any witnesses. The man I work for is not going to be happy about this. But all he cares about is the insurance money. It would have been perfect if you hadn't been here, but ..." The voice paused, "... maybe this will be better. Yeah! They'll think you started the fire and in your hurry to get out before anyone discovered you, you fell and hit your head and died here."

We peered inside to see a large man holding a crowbar in one hand and a flashlight in the other. He must have used the bar to pry off the padlock. He shined the light in Andy's face. Andy cowered in the corner. Behind us, the fire was growing in intensity.

"Just hold still, kid, and it'll make this a lot easier." The big man sounded congenial despite his intentions to commit murder.

He raised the crowbar to bludgeon Andy to death.

"Stop!" Willie yelled. The man spun on us, still holding the bar aloft. Suddenly, he tossed it away and reached under his jacket, pulling out a pistol.

"Now this does complicate things." His good-natured tone turned sour.

He motioned for us to join Andy, "Get over there."

He reached around by the door, lifted a metal can, and shook it. The label read 'Kerosene' and it was empty. He tossed it aside as if he was disappointed at the empty can.

"All right, walk through that door. I'll just have to make do."

He waved the gun towards the hallway. Andy went first but stopped inside the door and whirled.

"I know who you are ... you're uh ... you're Hal ... something! You were working here on this house! But you quit! You said you didn't want to be next! You're the one that went to the newspaper!"

"You talk too much, kid. Besides, my name's not really Hal. Move along now, like a good boy."

"What are you going to do with us?" I questioned. My fear grew as the fire got hotter and closer.   How ironic that for the first time since we left the roller rink, I was finally warm.

"I guess I can't worry about how it'll look now.   You're all in the way and I'm behind schedule. I can't leave any witnesses!"

He stepped closer and prodded me along. We turned down the hallway behind the kitchen. Willie and Andy walked beside each other, then me, followed by the arsonist.   I saw the scaffolding and quickly began forming a plan.

"There's a cellar up here and you three are going down into it. They'll find your bones in a few days if they ever clean up the ashes."

Andy stopped suddenly. He was right in front of the weakened floorboards.

"I don't wanna burn up! I'm not going any farther!" He screamed.

Willie stepped around the flooring and went a bit farther.

"Hold on there, you!" he ordered Willie. The man sounded frustrated.

I moved out of the way.

"And you," he addressed Andy, "get going!"

He stepped up to give Andy a shove, but just as he did, Andy side stepped and dived under the scaffolding. He got up suddenly and rocked it towards the man whose foot broke through the rotten floor boards. Bricks rained down, several of them hitting the man about the shoulders and head and coming very close to me. Suddenly, the scaffolding fell towards the man, pinning him to the floor. In the chaos, he dropped the gun when his elbow hit the floor, and I kicked it out of the way. By now, the flames were licking at the walls behind us.

"We've gotta get back to the kitchen!" Andy shouted.

"Hurry!" Willie hollered.

I went to follow, but as I did, the floorboard beneath me gave way and my right leg broke through. I felt something tear in my ankle and the rest of me fell forward, knocking out my breath.

"Help! Help!" called the man behind me. "Please! I'm trapped! I can't move ... please! For the love of God, help me!"

I tried to pry myself out of the hole. Willie and Andy were there in an instant. Willie grabbed me under the arms and pulled up while Andy tried to guide my leg. It seemed like forever as I watched the flames growing closer. But within seconds they had me extricated.

"Let's go!" Willie yelled.

But I couldn't put any weight on my ankle. The man behind us continued to plead for help.

"Please, oh please, help me! Look, I'm sorry, ok? You can call the cops when we get out. I'll go to jail. Just don't let me burn to death!"

"Come on, Andy!" I screamed.

But Andy turned back and looked at the man on the floor under the scaffold.

"Get her out of here!" he shouted, "I'm gonna help him."

Willie looked at me.

"Put your arms around my neck!" He commanded. I did and he quickly swept me up in his arms and ran.

We passed so near the flames I feared we would catch fire or he would trip and we would fall into it. But his feet were swift and sure and we made it past the flames and through the kitchen. The back door stood open and Willie ran through it and down the great stone steps that led to the carriage house and lawn.

The air outside was at once frigid. Willie carried me a good distance away from the mansion before he set me down. I tried to stand with my weight on my left foot, balancing. He turned back to the house and we both waited for Andy. Flames leapt through the windows towards the front of the house. Behind us I could just make out a dark automobile parked behind the carriage house, and noticed that the trunk was open.

"Come on, Andy," Willie urged.

In the distance I heard the wail of sirens. We were on the back side of the house. We waited a few seconds more and he turned to me.

"I've gotta go back."

I knew he did and I nodded. He slipped his jacket off and tenderly placed it around my shoulders.

I watched him as he turned back to the house, took a few steps, and stopped. He looked as if he'd forgotten something. He stared straight ahead and I wondered if he was reconsidering going back. When all at once, he whirled around and ran to me. He took my face in his hands, looked into my eyes, and pressed his lips to mine in a brief but firm kiss. Then he raced back to the house and ran inside without a word of goodbye.

Chapter Twenty-seven

I was dazed, stunned! I felt as if I couldn't breathe. I wanted to cry and I wanted to sing. But when I looked at the inferno he had entered, I couldn't do either. I collapsed on the ground and stared at the blaze as windows exploded and smoke billowed from them. Tears formed in my eyes as I prayed that God wouldn't let them die.

The sirens grew louder and around the corner of the house I could see a revolving red light. Within moments, two fire trucks were on the scene, racing up the driveway and stopping. Men in big coats and black firemen's helmets jumped out and started pulling out hoses from the backs of the trucks.

Someone hollered, "Over there! There's someone over there!"

"Please, Lord, bring them out alive," I pleaded out loud.

"Miss ... Miss!" A middle aged fireman peered down at me.

I looked up at him.

"Did you say there's somebody in there?"

"Three people! There ... by the kitchen!" I pointed urgently, "You have to go in that back door!"

He ran back to the engine shouting orders, "Bring that hose over here!"

I watched as they sprayed water over, and around the door through which Willie had passed only moments before. It was engulfed in flames.

"What's your name?" someone asked. I stared at the door, willing both boys to come through it.

"Hildi."

Two firemen charged through the door.

"Hildi. Is that a first name or a last name?"

"My name's Hildi, Hilda Barnum."

I watched two more firemen enter the house.

"This looks painful. How did it happen?"

I gasped suddenly. A searing pain shook me away from watching the house burn. A man was pouring liquid over the nasty scrape on my right   shin.

"I stepped on a rotten board and twisted my

ankle. There's a man in there and he set the fire! He said something about insurance ... that he's working for somebody who wants the insurance. I think that might be his car over there. He said he was going to kill us because we saw him." I was growing impatient. No one had come back out, "Look, there are people still in there!"

I finally shifted my attention to the person treating my leg. His eyes were kind and concerned.

"They are doing all they can to find them. And you do what you can out here ..." He opened his coat to reveal a clerical collar. "and so will I."

He took my hands and we bowed our heads together as he prayed.

"Precious Lord, hear us. We pray your hand would be on our friends right now, that you would protect them as you protected your children in the fiery furnace. And, Lord, I ask that you comfort Hildi, here. In Jesus' name, amen."

When we finished, I looked back toward the kitchen door again.

"They're coming out!" Another fireman announced.

I looked at the man, "Please, let me go to them!"

The fireman lifted me up easily, "I'll help you."

He put his arm around me.

"I'm Pastor James Philips, from the Congregational Church here in Ridgeview. We're all volunteers, every one of us. Were you at the skating rink tonight?"

I nodded.

"I was there for a bit at the beginning, but my daughter and my wife are both down with nasty colds, so I didn't stay."

The first two firemen began to emerge, each carrying a body over his shoulder. I let go of Pastor Philips and tried to run, but fell.

"Here, now, Hildi. I'll get you there." He picked me up and carried me to within a few yards of where the men were putting their burdens down.

I recognized Andy and Willie right away. Willie sat on the ground, his body convulsing in coughs. Andy lay nearby but wasn't moving. The right sleeve of his wool jacket was burned and smoking. Two more firemen came out carrying a much larger body between them. It was the man who had set the fire.

"Get the ambulance up here!" one of the men called.

One of the firemen had a metal canister that looked like something a scuba diver might use. He turned a knob on its top and put something over Willie's face. "Here, breathe this, son." Willie took hold of the mask and tried to breathe deeper.

More time was taken with Andy. A mask from the canister was put over his face and what I later learned was oxygen, turned on. In moments, Andy began to cough and soon he revived.

Another canister was taken to the man who had set the fire.

I again asked for the pastor to get me nearer. He carried me up to the coughing boys and set me down.

"This guy's not coming around." The man who set the fire didn't look good.

Willie couldn't talk but looked at me over the oxygen mask. Andy's arm was badly burned. The firemen had removed his wool jacket and were examining him.

Before the ambulance arrived, the sheriff came. Melvin Steele almost didn't recognize me.

"Well, Hildi Barnum? I thought you'd had your fill of excitement and danger!"

"Hello, Sheriff." I answered, sheepishly.

He crouched on the ground next to me. "All right. What happened here? Why were the four of you in a house that's supposed to be locked up?"

I explained our going to the house, why Andy was there, and how he discovered the man setting it on fire. I pointed out the car and the sheriff checked it out. Inside was another can of kerosene.

"I think you might have just answered some questions we've needed some answers to. I'm going to head over to my office and make a phone call. I've got someone for you to talk to when he gets here. He's staying at the hotel."

The sheriff walked back to his car and drove off. The ambulance was already there. They loaded up the man who was still unconscious and sped off. Blankets were brought and placed around the boys' shoulders. They were given water to drink and a wet rag to wipe the soot from their faces.

Willie lifted the oxygen mask and looked at me.

"Want to know?" He finally asked.

"Want to know what?"

"What I told Betty?" He coughed a little after he posed the question.

I'd forgotten all about skating, all about the excitement of the night before we left the roller rink and came to this place.

"What did you tell her?"

"I told her ... I was taking you out for the night ... and not to expect us back until ..." He stopped and looked into my eyes, "... until I gave you something."

"What's that?" I wondered.

"... *Your* first kiss, Hildi ... I'm sorry. It wasn't exactly how I'd planned it. But I had to do it ... in case I didn't get out."

Another ambulance arrived shortly and took Andy away. Just after it left, his brothers came running up to where we were.

"What happened?" Gabe demanded, scanning the grounds.

"Oh, no!" Sam cried, growing hysterical "No, no, no! Where is he? Andy ... he's dead isn't he? He's gotta be! Oh, God, no! Please, God, no!"

How strange, I thought, as I wondered if this was an expression of grief, or if he was calling on the God of the universe to do something to save the brother he had locked in what had turned into an inferno.

Sam collapsed on the ground and sobbed, beating the dirt with his fists. Gabe wandered around emotionless, but he was murmuring something that rose to a crescendo.

"We never shoulda ... never ... never, never ... We never shoulda done this! This is on you! This is on you, Sam! This was your idea and now you killed our brother!" Gabe piled onto Sam who was still on the ground and started throwing punches.

"Hey! Break it up!" A couple of firemen were there, pulling the two apart. "Break it up, I said! What is wrong with you?"

Sam sobbed, "Our little brother was in there!"

The fireman put a hand on Sam's shoulder, "Blond kid?"

Gabe nodded.

"He's going to be just fine. He has a bad burn on his arm and took in a lot of smoke, though. He was trying to get someone else out. If the other guy survives, your brother probably helped to save his life."

The fireman guided Andy's brothers back towards the street where onlookers had gathered to watch the blaze.

I turned back to Willie, "What happened in there?"

He lifted the mask and spoke between coughs, "Somehow Andy and I got the scaffolding off that guy. I don't know how we did it 'cause it was really heavy. The two of us tried to pull him out, but it was so hot and smoky we couldn't breathe. The next thing I know, I'm out here."

Sheriff Steele returned shortly with another person in his police car. This fellow looked a bit familiar as he walked up to us. His hair was gray and he wore a sports coat over what appeared to be a pajama top. He peered down at us through tired eyes.

"Hildi, Willie, this is Howard Buckley. He's an investigator for an insurance company and has some questions for you."

At once, I recognized the other man, the fisherman from the day we ran into the Porters.

"I think we've met before," Buckley remarked with a knowing look then turned to Steele. "I was doing a little fly fishing when I met these two."

"Down in the Ottertail," Willie answered. "Did you get your carp smoked?"

Buckley nodded, "It was like you said. We traded what we caught for some that were already smoked. That was good advice, son. Now, back to the matter at hand. This fellow who set the fire, he said he was working for someone? What exactly did he say?"

We recounted what we heard outside the kitchen door. Buckley and Steele listened intently.

"We've suspected Dobkins of insurance fraud. He has properties all over the tri-state area and in the last year and a half, three of them have 'mysteriously' caught fire. The insurance payouts have been pretty steep. He would insure these properties for the value they would fetch once the renovations were complete. When we trace the license plates on the car, I'm pretty sure we'll find out that they belong to a thug named Jimmy O'Rourke. His friends call him 'Jimmy the Torch'. The police haven't been able to get anything on the 'Torch' and nothing to tie him to Dobkins. With him in the hospital, a car full of kerosene cans, and your testimony, I think they'll finally have a case."

Willie shook his head, "No, that can't be right. Andy said he recognized him, that this man worked for his dad. He called him 'Hal'."

"But you see, that's how he operates. What we know about Jimmy is this: he passes himself off as a local carpenter or whatever the mark is looking for. He gives 'em a phony name. He gets himself hired, learns the layout of the land, and then pretends to get hurt or sick so he has to quit. When he's sure he won't be suspected, he does the job and torches the place."

I remembered the big man's pleas for help, the firemen carrying him out, and how he laid so still on the ground.

"Do you think he'll live?" I asked.

Buckley pulled out a pack of cigarettes, took one out and tapped it lightly on the pack. "I hope so. It's hard to tell. The sheriff, here, says he's not good. People can die of smoke inhalation."

Buckley put the cigarette in his mouth but didn't light it. He looked at Willie, "How 'bout you, Will? 'Suppose I can't smoke now if you're sucking on that oxygen. You need to go in?"

Willie shook his head. "No, I'm not going to the hospital. I'm all right. But Hildi hurt her ankle."

I joined Willie in not wanting to go to the hospital. "It's just a sprain. I want to go back to the roller rink."

Willie nodded in agreement.

Sheriff Steele looked like he was about to overrule us, but I jumped in. "If I'd sprained my ankle at the roller rink I wouldn't be going to the hospital."

He smoothed the thin mustache above his lip. "Get in the car and we'll drop you off."

Chapter Twenty-eight

I guess we didn't look too bad for having gone through a fire and an attack by a thug. My pretty blue dress didn't appear to have suffered, and Pastor Philips had done a good job of cleaning up my scraped shin with what he had available. After applying three or four Band-Aids, you couldn't even see it. He taped up my swollen ankle and I was able to bear weight and walk on it without much of a limp.

It was two in the morning when the squad car pulled up to an open spot along the curb. There were still quite a few cars along the street outside the roller rink, but there were also many open spots that hadn't been there when we left. We thanked the sheriff for the ride and waved at Mr. Buckley, then started up the sidewalk.

No kids milled around outside as they had before and when we entered the building, we noticed that slightly more than half the group remained. This provided many more open tables and chairs. Only a few people skated and the organ was silent. In the corner, behind the food table, I saw Kathy asleep with her head on Larry's shoulder. He appeared to be dozing, too. The one person who looked to be wide awake was Willie's sister, Betty, and when she spotted us, she made a bee-line for us.

"Where have you been?" her eyes were wide with concern even though her tone sounded irritated. "I was just about to say something to Kathy about sending Larry out to find you. Do you realize you've been gone for nearly three hours? Willie?"

She noticed my limp and glanced down at my leg, "You've been up to something, haven't you. I can't believe this!"

We slowly made our way to a table. Betty and I sat down.

"I think we're done skating for the night." Willie found our skates, turned them in, and headed for the food table.

"What happened, Hildi?"

I explained the last three hours. My story was accompanied by gasps of shock and sounds of disbelief by a big sister who was clearly angry with yet another dangerous situation in which her little brother found himself.

Finally, when I had finished my oration, Betty put a hand to her forehead in a gesture that said, 'Lord, give me strength!'

"This is not what he told me! I swear, my brother thinks he is indestructible! You know what he told me?" She stopped suddenly and gave me a look of pity. "... Oh, never mind!"

Willie returned with a plate of sandwiches and bars and two glasses of punch. He put one glass in front of me, but the plate he placed in front of himself and dived in.

"I'm starved!" he said and stuffed his mouth with a sandwich.

Betty's eyes narrowed, "You are in so much trouble!"

"You told her?" He asked with a mouthful of food and I nodded.

"I'm sorry."'

He shrugged and kept eating, "It's all right. Better coming from you than from me. Whenever I have to explain myself to Betty, she interrupts me. It's like I've got two mothers!"

She glared and shook her head at him. But he went on.

"We were just going to check on Andy, but things happened and we ended up staying longer. Betty, these things were weird, out of the ordinary. I can't explain the shadow of a noose appearing and disappearing. There were other things that happened. And if we hadn't stayed, I think Andy would have been killed."

She sat back and stared at him, her features softening. At last, she spoke, "I love you, little brother, but I swear you're going to give me gray hair before I turn twenty!"

The rest of the evening I sat with my ankles on Willie's knees. Our table was in the corner with a wall right behind each of our two chairs. It was easy to lean back and rest my head against the wall and I was not terribly uncomfortable. We didn't speak of the kiss, but I ran it through my mind at least a dozen times. Eventually, I dozed off and when I awoke, the rink was nearly empty.

"Hildi," Willie's voice croaked. He cleared it and tried again, "Hildi wake up. Your pa's here."

My eyelids were heavy, my back ached, and I could feel that my ankle had swollen while I slept and was pressing against the wrapping that had been applied four and a half hours earlier. I took a deep breath and stretched. Daddy spotted us and walked over to our table.

"Ready to go? Let's see, I'm supposed to have two more Coopers." He looked around the silent rink. Just about everyone was gone so it was easy to locate Kathy and Betty. The trick would be getting Kathy to shorten her goodbyes to Larry.

Daddy gestured to the two girls that he was in a hurry.

"Come on, kids, let's go."

I stood but the mobility I'd gained earlier was gone and I could barely put any weight on my ankle again. Daddy noticed the bandage peeking out from under my sock and the scrape beneath the band-aids on my shin. He shook his head and clucked his tongue.

"No wonder you don't like to skate if you fall that hard!"

Daddy helped me up and put an arm around me as I limped outside. The others followed, including Larry.

"This isn't from skating," I confessed.

Daddy's eyebrows went up and he looked down at me.

"Well, I can't wait to hear about it."

Chapter Twenty-nine

This time, I sat in the front seat while Willie and his sisters rode in the back. Daddy wasn't kidding about wanting to hear about my twisted ankle. It was still fairly dark outside with just a glimmer of light on the eastern horizon. Once we dropped into the valley, that glow would disappear behind the bluffs. The dash lights were bright, though, and I could see Daddy's expression as we traveled.

"So, if you didn't do that on the rink, how'd it happen? Did you trip walking into the joint?" I knew his casual tone and smile wouldn't last long.

"Not exactly. It's kind of complicated," I began.

I knew I had to be honest. It would have been tempting to leave out some details like the fact that Willie didn't want me to go. I told the important parts. But the part about what happened in the attic and how Willie gave me my first kiss were left out. Nevertheless, I could see Willie in the rear-view mirror and he looked like he wanted to crawl under the seat. I caught Daddy glancing in the rear-view mirror, too, and this was the first time he actually looked angry with my best friend.

"You make sure you tell your dad about this, son ... or I will," Daddy's tone was stern as he addressed Willie.

Willie swallowed hard and responded, "Yes, sir."

Most of the drive home was done in silence. I knew I was in trouble again. I knew Willie would 'get it' and I remembered Chet's warning to his son before going inside the rink. But it wasn't like we were looking for trouble. And we hadn't planned on staying so long. We hadn't planned on nearly being burned to death.

Daddy dropped off the Coopers and soon we were driving down our own long driveway. The rays of sun were just peeking over the bluffs and cast a yellow sheen on our big white farm house. In that light, his eyes softened a bit and he looked at me and smiled.

"Did you have fun skating tonight? Was it as bad as you thought it would be?"

I thought back on Willie guiding me around the rink and the couples' skate, the low lights, the kiss outside the burning house. Despite the drama there, I couldn't help the thrill I felt.

"Yes, Daddy, it was wonderful!"

He turned serious, but not angry. "You know we'll have some things to discuss after I fill in your mother on what happened tonight."

"I know," I answered.

He parked the car and turned in his seat, "You go inside and get a little more sleep. We'll talk about this later."

I knew the wait would be harder than facing the consequences right away. But, I was tired, and my ankle throbbed. I could stand a little more sleep.

The ring of the telephone woke me at 8:45. At least I had a couple hours of rest before the talk. My ankle ached. I took off the tape the fireman had applied earlier. I changed into my everyday clothes, freshened up in the bathroom, and headed downstairs with a limp.

I could hear Mom talking to someone on the telephone, so I went to the kitchen and sat at the table to await my fate. I thought about my defense but knew I'd better keep it to myself. My folks were fair, but they were not open to hear appeals from the accused. I knew that whatever was about to be decreed was sealed.   Any investigation into what had transpired would have been completed. Then the two would sit together and agree on a consequence. My parents were the perfect team, always united. Several times my brothers had attempted to play one parent against another, but with no success.

"Good morning, Sunshine," Mom's greeting didn't quite go with the look in her eyes or the tone of her voice. It was one of those 'mom' looks that said she knew she was looking at the person who had broken her priceless vase. I hadn't broken a vase, but maybe I had broken a trust.

"Hi," I responded.

She opened the back door and pulled in a wooden crate containing several large squash. I could tell it was heavy by the way it scraped on the floor. The large gourds inside were clean on the top and muddy on the bottom.

"Well," she began, "first things first, your father and I are glad you were honest about leaving the roller skating rink and going to the Crenshaw house. We're also very relieved that you don't have more than a sore ankle. However, ..."

I could already tell I was in trouble when she referred to Daddy as 'your father', but when she added the 'however', I dreaded what was to follow.

"... that doesn't mean that we can forget the matter. We were under the impression that you knew you were to stay with the group last night. For future reference, *if* we ever let you go to something like this again, it is to be understood that you *will* stay with the group from the time you are dropped off until you are picked up. Furthermore, you will be spending the next week doing your chores and your sister's chores and that includes cleaning and cutting up these squash for canning today. You didn't exactly do anything wrong, Hildi, but we think you used poor judgment.

"And that brings me to the realization that it is time you and I have a talk that maybe we should have had a long time ago. I know what is going on in here, Hildi."

Mom put a hand over her heart and gazed compassionately into my eyes, "I know why you went to the Crenshaw house. Not because Willie asked you to go, but because you wanted to be with him. I've noticed how you light up when he is around, how you look at him. Your feelings towards him aren't the way they were a year ago. That means your decisions are clouded by your feelings. I won't tell you that this is puppy love and that it will pass away because I don't know. It's different for everyone. But I will tell you that you have to be very careful. Instead of thinking things through and weighing the consequences, you'll be tempted to do things according to how you feel. Do you understand what I'm saying?"

I nodded that I understood. And that was when my mother gave me *'the talk'*, the *'birds and the bees'* talk! Now, I was a farm girl and I knew all about how baby animals were made. I'd even helped cows give birth. And I'd heard Stella Johnson talk about things like this and she didn't leave anything out. So, I really didn't learn much more than what I already knew. And yet, my mother in her wisdom reminded me that we aren't animals and the things we talked about were to take place within the bonds of marriage. She wanted me to understand that being 'in love' is not an excuse for making bad decisions, for not controlling one's urges. And although she again stated what I had heard so often, that they all loved Willie, he was human and the nature of man is fallen. Even a strong Christian could be tempted and fail.

When the talk was over, when Mom had dispensed her wisdom and advice and after she had admonished me for my poor judgment, she stood up and embraced me.

"Hilda, you're turning into a beautiful young lady, do you know that?" She held me at arm's length and looked at me.

I knew that, as my mom, I would be beautiful *to her* ...

Chapter Thirty

Late October had its extremes: hot, Indian summer days as well as cool and downright cold days. The tobacco in the sheds was turning rich golden browns, and the aroma as it cured was pleasant as it wafted past us on a light breeze. As soon as we had a foggy, drizzly day, we would take it down and pile the speared lathes of tobacco in the shed where it would sit until we were ready to strip off the leaves and put them into fifty-pound bales. I looked forward to the next phase of the tobacco harvest where we would again share work with our neighbors. When we started 'stripping tobacco', that is, stripping the leaves off the stalks and putting them into bales, it would mean fun nights of visiting and listening to the radio in the barn. My favorite part of stripping tobacco was jumping up and down on the bales to compress the leaves. We would move some of the tobacco to one end of our dairy barn where it was warm and commence that part of the harvest there. Granddad and Grandma would come down and we'd listen to the radio while we worked. When our hands got cold, we'd find a warm place for them. My favorite place was between one of the cow's hind legs and her udder. At first her eyes would get wide and she'd dance around a little, but soon she would go back to chewing her cud and accept the intrusion. Once my hands were warm, I'd go back to work.

The Monday back to school after the weekend All-Night Skating event was crisp, and we dressed in layers in case it warmed up during the course of the day. My ankle was still swollen and stiff and it made me wonder how Andy was. I thought back to the blackened sleeve of his jacket and how some of the material of his shirt seemed to cling to the burn. He and his mother didn't show up for church, and I wondered if that meant that the burn was so painful that it kept him home, or if they only meant to come that one time. I thought about his brothers and if they realized how brave Andy had been. Did they feel any guilt at all for putting him in that kind of danger? Did they give him any credit for what he had done? He stayed behind to help a stranger who just moments before had said he intended to kill us.

It took me a little longer to walk the two miles to school. Even my brothers and sister didn't wait for me, so I was one of the last ones to arrive. When I got inside, I saw that Andy and Willie were both there and everyone was gathered around Andy. He had a large gauze bandage around his right forearm that stretched from just behind his wrist to just below his elbow.

"What's going on?" I asked.

My sister answered, "Andy's telling us about what happened at the Crenshaw house!"

I pushed into the crowd in order to hear what was being said.

"... So this guy's on the floor and screaming for help. I told Cooper to get Hildi out and then I tried to lift the scaffolding off of him, but it was too heavy. I knew right away that there wasn't any way I could do it alone, but I kept trying. After a while, Cooper comes back and the two of us try to lift it, and the fire's falling all around us, and I'm thinkin' maybe this is what hell's like. The guy on the floor passed out and the smoke is gettin' so thick we can't even see each other. I can hear Cooper prayin' over there, then all of a sudden, the scaffold budges and we're able to get it up! We both grab this guy and try to move him, but he's too heavy. We're pushing and pulling and coughing. My eyes are stinging and I can't breathe. Next thing I know, I'm waking up outside next to Cooper!"

"Wow! How did you get out? What about the other guy?" Questions came from all over the classroom.

Stella Johnson was nearly draping herself over Andy, "You were so brave!"

He held up a hand to quiet them down and turned slightly away from Stella, "The other guy was in bad shape with some really bad burns on his back and hands. He was unconscious from the time they brought him out of the house until he came around yesterday and confessed everything. I guess he's cooperating with some investigator, so they won't need our testimony. And how'd we get out? The firemen hauled us out. Just before I passed out, the fire was all around us. The firemen said they couldn't understand why I wasn't burned worse. I shoulda had more burns than this." He referred to the bandaged arm. "Cooper wasn't burnt at all. They said that with how intense the fire was, both of us should either be dead or burned beyond help."

I wondered.

"Anyway, the Crenshaw house is nothing but a shell now. We moved out here because my pop thought we might be in danger, what with the strange things that happened at the house. Now, he's pretty sure it was that guy in the hospital. It sounds like we'll be moving back to our house in Ridgeveiw probably in the next week or so."

Miss Hendricks tapped her ruler on the desk. "I hate to break this up but it's time to start. Please take your places. Whose turn is it to lead the Pledge of Allegiance?"

Right away I could see a change for the better in Andy. As the week progressed, I noticed that he spent a lot more time with Willie, which meant that I didn't. But I knew that this was a good thing. I spent time with my sister and the other girls at school; Willie and I would probably catch up later.

And true to his word, the Porter family returned to their home in Ridgeview by November. An article in the paper reported that Herschel Dobkins had been indicted for insurance fraud and conspiracy to commit arson as well as several other charges which extended to the other properties Mr. Buckley had told us about that night. 'Jimmy the Torch' turned state's evidence, giving the law all they needed for the indictment. At first, Dobkins wanted the Torch to make it look like the fire was an accident or a result of some kind of 'paranormal' activity. But as his arguments with Rueben Porter began to escalate, he wanted Jimmy to see if he could make it look like the fire was set by the disgruntled contractor. Dobkins had already taken in nearly a hundred thousand dollars in insurance payouts on the other houses he had burned. Buckley couldn't have been happier that he had his man.

Chapter Thirty-one

I wasn't alone as I dressed. Lila was sleeping soundly on the other side of the room and I had to be very careful or I might wake her and have to explain what I was doing. The only light in the bedroom was a ghostly pale light from the moon high above the valley floor which seemed larger than I had ever seen it.

I looked at the note again.

Meet me on the bluff at midnight.

Willie passed it to me during Sunday school. It wasn't like we weren't paying attention. He snuck it under my Bible. Why all the secrecy? I didn't know. But what leapt into my mind was the talk Mom had with me a few weeks earlier. I had gone to the Crenshaw house to be with Willie. My feelings had changed from friendship to something deeper. She had warned me that my judgment might be clouded by my feelings. I needed to stop and think, to weigh the consequences of my actions. And yet, I still decided to go.

It would take me a good ten minutes to get to the base of the bluff and another fifteen minutes for the climb. I heard the mantle clock below strike the half hour, 11:30. I was getting good at sneaking out, but once outside, I was in trouble. There was movement in the doorway of the barn and I knew that I had been discovered. In an instant, our new border collie pup, Honey, sprang out of the barn and was nipping at my shoestrings and jumping about. I knelt down and rubbed her head and back. She was nearly four months old now but still had her silky puppy fur.

"What are you doing up?" I whispered hoarsely, "Here, let's go back to the barn." Before I grabbed her collar, Honey gave me a wet doggy kiss on the face.

I gave her another pet and a hug. Maybe that was a mistake, for no sooner had I shut her inside than the barking began, and it was not soft barking. This was loud, mournful doggy pleading. Mom and Daddy's bedroom was on the side of the house facing the barn and I knew that Daddy did not need much of a reason to get up and go to the barn to check strange sounds.

I opened the door and Honey stopped her wailing.

"Honey!" I whispered as harshly as I could, "Lay down and be quiet."

Of course, she understood everything I said, so I shut the door only to find that she ignored my orders. I opened the door again and she stopped, looked at me, and cocked her head. She had a broad smile on her face and wagged her tail. She trotted out the door and sat down beside me. I grabbed her collar and drug her back inside the barn, slamming the door; but immediately, the howling commenced again.

My battle with the pup continued until I finally conceded that she had won and would accompany me on my midnight trek. The look I got said 'what are you waiting for?' I quickly snatched some binder twine that dad kept hanging inside the barn door, looped it through her collar and took off at a trot to make up for the time I'd lost.

Pups are not easy to lead. In fact, half way to the bluff Honey decided she needed a rest. She sat. I pulled and reluctantly she came, but the tension on the twine told me that this would not be easy. I soon found out how hard it would be when I was forced to carry her up the steepest parts of the bluff. I had no light except for the brilliant moon, but there was a glimmer overhead as I strained up at the rock face of the bluff. It was a flashlight and I knew it was Willie who held it. I shifted Honey in my arms; her fur was soft and smelled like new mown hay. The most difficult part of the climb was the last few yards. We were at the base of the bluff, just below the big rock that jutted out over the valley, lending itself to a commanding view. Above me, I thought I could make out the outline of a person and I knew that Willie was waiting.

I unzipped my jacket and shoved my now 'floppy' puppy inside. She was a bit big to carry inside my coat, but the hike had worn her out, so she was ready to be still and accepted my pushing her into the space I'd created. I zipped the jacket back up, leaving just her head out, and began the familiar but treacherous climb up the rugged rocks. My passenger didn't help things because right before I reached the top, she began to whine and try to wriggle free. This could have ended in disaster, but in an instant, Willie was there hauling me up.

"You brought Honey with you?" He asked when I let her out of my coat.

I could see him clearly in the moonlight. "I didn't have a choice. She saw me and started barking. I was afraid Daddy would hear and I wouldn't get to come."

Willie sounded irritated when he noticed my dog, but when I answered, I saw that he had her on his lap, rubbing her ears.

"Her fur is so soft," he said and she licked his face to show him she didn't hold any hard feelings towards him.

The very top of the bluff was bare limestone with a few mossy and grassy spots. It overlooked the length of our valley, and at night it was exciting to see the few lights from the farms that were scattered on the valley floor and also on the opposing hilltops. I sat down next to Willie who still petted the pup.

"What's the big mystery?" I asked, referring to his note.

He shook his head in the moonlight, "No mystery. I just didn't want anybody getting the wrong idea about me asking you up here so late at night."

I didn't know if I liked that.

"Andy called today." He remarked offhandedly.

"He did? How is he? Does he like being back in Ridgeview or does he miss us 'hicks?'"

I could see Willie's grin in the moonlight, "He accepted the Lord today, Hildi. He was baptized after church!"

"Oh, Willie!" I cried, "That's wonderful!"

"And he said that the rest of his family was there to see it."

My mind instantly took me back to those conversations we had, walking home from church that Sunday nearly two months ago, and the other one we had after the beating Mr. Arnold had given him. And now he was so excited and so happy. In time, I would learn that Willie had spent time telling Andy about the Lord, that is, after Andy told him he was ready to hear it. My friend had made a sacrifice, and he'd made a difference.

"Look up, Hildi," Willie said, and when I did, I saw a shooting star. And not just one. All across the heavens were streaks of light, some faint and some bright.

"It's a meteor shower! Miss Hendricks told me about it. It doesn't happen too often but this is the best time of night to see one."

I scanned the sky as I watched another and then another arc across the sky. A couple of summers ago we had watched lightning on the horizon and 'ooed' and 'awed' like we were watching fireworks. That night we sat on a load of newly bailed hay. It had been hot and we were worn out from loading bails. But this night was cold with the chilly bite of late autumn and my feelings were all a-jumble as I tried to watch the stars and not worry about what to say or how to act. My neck was becoming stiff as I sat looking up, and soon I lay back on the cold stone of the bluff and watched in silence with Willie beside me and Honey in between.

I don't know how long we watched the stars, but my body was beginning to react to the frosty air. I could feel myself trembling in my clothes. I sat up and pulled the pup onto my lap.

"You're cold," Willie remarked.

I nodded. And then he did something I didn't expect. He scooted up close behind me, opened his coat, and wrapped it and his arms around me. It was warm inside and I could feel my trembling grow less and less.

At first I was nervous. I didn't know what I was supposed to do or what he meant by it, but Willie seemed strong and sure of himself and as I became comfortable and warm, I leaned back against him.

"Hildi," he said softly.

"What?"

"I wanted you to see this. I don't know, it just seemed like it would be better, watchin' this with you."

"Will?" I tried out the more mature sounding version of his name.

"Yeah?"

"Ramona Rawlins."

"Oh, her. I might as well tell you. Just before the skating thing, I sent her back that bracelet and a letter. I told her I wasn't her boyfriend ... that I never was her boyfriend. And that maybe there is someone else ... she hasn't written back and I haven't heard if she's killed herself yet."

I was silent, but I knew that if he could see my face, he'd see a grin that stretched from ear to ear. I didn't want to ruin this special time by saying what I was thinking. We sat for a while longer, watching the meteors cross the sky and sharing warmth inside his coat.

"It's probably time we head home." He pulled his jacket from around me and buttoned it back up. Then he stood and offered me his hand which had become a common gesture for him. I took it and he pulled me to my feet. I grabbed Honey's twine, but she sat down so I picked her up.

"Mind if I walk you home?" He asked.

"You don't have to," I wished I hadn't said it as soon as I had.

But he smiled and responded, "I know."

We took turns carrying the pup. The trip down the bluff is always quicker than going up except that one has to be careful not to lose his balance or get tangled in berry briars. If that happened, you might end up rolling down the hill and breaking your neck. Once down, it was a matter of crossing the creek by stepping on the strategically placed rocks by moonlight without getting our feet wet. In short, the twenty-five minute climb turned into a twenty minute descent.

The barn was dark and the calves asleep when I took Honey in and laid her next to Queenie. This time, she didn't make a fuss as I closed the door. The yard light glowed just enough for me to see from the barn to the front door. Thankfully, the house was still dark.

"Thank you," I said, "for showing me the shooting stars and walking me home."

"You're welcome." Willie replied. "C'mon."

He took my hand and walked me to the big elm in our front yard. The only light that touched this spot was the moonlight that streamed through the spreading branches of the tree. We stopped underneath it. He faced me and took both my hands in his.

"Remember the night of the fire? I gave you something, but I told you it wasn't how I'd planned it?"

I remembered the kiss he'd given me in haste before risking his life for Andy. I waited for him to go on.

"Well ... I wanted it to be something to remember and this is how it was supposed to go: After we checked on Andy I was going to walk you to the city park, and you know that big old oak tree in the middle of it?"

I nodded. The tree was known as the 'Lover's Tree' and it bore the initials of many couples who had carved them there over the years.

"That was where it was supposed to happen, underneath that big old tree, just the two of us, alone in the moonlight."

He stepped closer to me. My pulse quickened as he touched my face and lifted my chin towards him. He bent and his kiss was warm, soft, and lingering. When he stepped away, I knew that even if we weren't under the 'Lover's Tree', he had succeeded. Even if it was not my *first kiss* it was a kiss to remember.

"Hildi, you are my best friend and you mean a lot to me," he whispered. "You always keep me on track. You're the one who reminds me to keep my eyes on the Lord. No one, not Ramona Rawlins or anyone else, will ever take your place."

And with those words spoken in earnest, he took his flashlight out of his pocket, turned it on, and went home. I watched him until I couldn't see him anymore. It was late, we had school the next day, and I had to go in and go back to bed. But I didn't want this feeling ... no, this moment to end. I waited as long as I could, breathing the cold November air and reliving the bluff top and the kiss under the elm tree. At last, I succumbed to the tiredness creeping into my body. I successfully secreted my way back inside without alerting anyone. As I changed into my nightgown and slipped beneath the covers, I knew my sense of elation was going to keep me awake long after I hoped to be asleep. But eventually, I drifted off as I pondered whether or not this had been a date ... or a proposal.

***

It's funny how sometimes, after an event late in the evening, you wake up and wonder if your imagination has played a trick on you. There is no evidence of what transpired the night before that sent your heart sailing over the moon. Such was the case the next morning. I awoke in elation but couldn't tell anyone about watching the shooting stars on the bluff top or the kiss under the spreading elm tree.

November mornings are cold and dark. I dressed and went out to do my chores. On my way, I stopped a moment and stared at the elm tree in the darkness. Did it really happen? Did

Willie and I stand under this tree just a few hours earlier or was it all a dream? I didn't ponder too long but hurried to do my chores because I'd overslept by half an hour. For some reason, Lila let me sleep.

By 7:00 I was back in the house, cleaning up and getting ready for school. The bacon sizzled in the skillet. The smell of the bacon and brewing coffee mingled together and swept away any remnants of drowsiness that the cool morning air hadn't banished.

"Something's different," Lila remarked and looked at me with a skeptical eye.

"I don't know what you're talking about," I replied and sat down to tie my shoes.

But Lila was sharp, "No. You're not telling me something and I can see that you want to. Well, when you're ready, you know where you can find me."

She pulled on a sweater and headed down the stairs.

We ate quickly, grabbed our books and lunches, and went out the front door. The boys were in a hurry and ran up the driveway. Lila walked briskly ahead of me. The big elm stood as a silent witness to the night's event and again I stopped beside it. I looked at the grass and leaves beneath it where I thought we had stood and remembered the moment again. Then, slowly, I lifted my eyes to its great trunk and scanned its surface. Suddenly, something caught my eye and I stopped.

"C'mon, Hildi! Let's go!" Ben was down the driveway a bit with Joe right behind him. But Lila, who hadn't gone too far, returned and stood beside me.

"What is that?" she exclaimed softly.

There, carved on the surface of that elm tree was a heart and inside it, *"W.C. loves H.B."*

Acknowledgments

Thanks first to Andy Overett and Lighthouse Publishing. Thanks so much to Erin Muhs for her incredible cover art. My ongoing thanks to: Carolyn Sween, for her constant encouragement; to Sharon Thiel, for your insight; to Chris Detert for his help on the poster; and, especially, to Cheryl Moen for your editing skills and your wise counsel. I owe you a new red pen. My appreciation to Lexi, Keneshia, Lydia and Emily for checking out the manuscript and giving me a 'teen's perspective. Thanks always to my mother, Rosie Moe for raising us to know and love the Lord. Thanks to Aunt Barb, my best promoter; and Aunt Pat, the story-teller in the family. I am blessed with many friends and many family members who might have not had a direct hand in this work, but help to keep my life on track through what they do behind the scenes and at home: Paul, Roxie, Amber, Jade and Hunter. I love you all. Finally, there is only One who gives life and sustains it. To Him be all glory and honor. Praise God.